River

Chase

This Book is the Property of the Carole L. Bi—— 7/02/05

Ron Shepherd

PublishAmerica
Baltimore

First printing

ISBN: 1-4137-6404-5
PUBLISHED BY PUBLISHAMERICA, LLLP
www.publishamerica.com
Baltimore

Printed in the United States of America

✎To all of my kids, with love✎

-Table of Contents-

Preface

A large herd of caribou meandered slowly across the face of Gitche Manitou's creation, searching for lichens and small willow brush to sustain themselves. Once in a while, the lead bull would abruptly stop and raise his head, looking for anything that might be a threat to himself or his herd. His large black nose drew in the surrounding air, searching for the scent of wolves. His status in this group meant he was expected to keep an ever watchful eye out for danger. For several days this great herd of caribou had traversed the land, seeking a place suitable for calving.

Off in the distance, a small pack of wolves angled toward the herd, making them gather speed, moving them at a faster pace. To the lead bull, they were no more than specks on the tapestry of the open land. He could see what was happening, but it was too far away to concern him. The wolf pack picked out a small cow and tried over and over to separate her from the rest of the herd. When they at last succeeded, there was little she could do but run and run hard. If she faltered even for a moment, she would be in serious trouble.

The wolves took turns running alongside her and it appeared that she was about to be overtaken by the pack. In reality, they were doing nothing more than making her expend her energy. This continued for many minutes, the wolves playing out their most successful method of hunting. Her eyes bulged wide in fear and her mouth gaped open, trying desperately to take in as much air as her lungs could hold. She stumbled for just a second and the ever watchful pack saw the moment of weakness and were spurred on to continue the chase. There was a barely discernable stumble, her flanks heaving hard, gasping for air. This was the signal to the pack that their long awaited meal was at hand. The lead wolf ran up close and grabbed a mouthful of flank and hair, holding on, slowing her up. The rest of the pack was there in an instant and what happened to her next passed in a flurry of pain and snarling wolves. She was down on the ground with many animals tearing at her flesh. The big male had torn her flank and her entrails bulged from the wound. She was being devoured alive and then even that faded from importance and she was gradually transformed into food to keep the pack strong.

Once the herd saw that the cow had been singled out, they rested easy. Today was not their day to die. They continued to walk along, looking for anything edible with no regard for their fallen comrade.

The herd moved into a draw that lead to an ancient river crossing, a place many herds used while heading to spring grazing grounds. The animals all felt a bit on edge, because their usual escape routes, their open country where they could see for so far, was now reduced to a narrow spot barely a hundred feet across. Ahead they could see the river, and from there on it would be easy going for many weeks. It was now a time for dropping new calves, and many predators followed them hoping for an easy meal. Winter had been hard on the entire herd, with many falling to starvation and determined enemies. They could almost smell the green grass yet to come. Their eyes rolled back and forth in their heads, searching for trouble. The entire herd was making a low grumbling sound, an indication that they were not at peace with their situation. As they moved uneasily, they made a clicking sound each time one of them took a step, the sound of leg tendons snapping across their joints.

━━ ━━ ━━

Earlier in the morning a young man wearing the hide of an animal had run breathless into the cave, waving his arms wildly and making some sort of talk that none could understand. He came to winter with this clan when he had become lost in a snow storm. The language was strange to the cave-dwellers and not much of what he said was understood by them. He was young and impatient and tried over and over to tell of what he had seen. He took the oldest man, a clan member of perhaps thirty summers, and pulled him to the cave wall. Over and over he pointed at the image of a caribou that was drawn on the wall with a fire-blackened stick. He would point at the animal and then run to the cave opening, gesturing wildly, pointing off to the west.

After doing this several times, the message he was trying so desperately to convey was understood. The elder grabbed his spear and, pointing with it westward, said something like "washka.." Then the clansmen all understood. The young message-bringer had seen a herd of caribou.

There were preparations to be made. Winter had been a

time of making weapons and trying to stay warm. Their food was nearly gone and they had resorted to boiling pieces of animal hides to eat. Water heated with hot rocks was the preferred method of boiling things. Now the time of plenty was once more nearly upon them.

The messenger lead the clan to where he had seen the animals and by evening they had spotted them moving toward the river. There were several hundred animals, but it would be no easy task to kill one. They were fierce animals in a fight.

The leader of the clan had hunted here several times before and his plan was the same as the one he had been taught when he was small. When the herd passed into the narrow place, several men would form a line so they couldn't go back the way they had came. They would try to stampede the herd into the water. Then as a good many animals passed the first hunters, the line would be drawn and the men would come with their burning torches, chasing the herd hard toward the river. The rest of the men would wait near the water for the caribou to pass in front of them.

Ahead, the men were ready. The caribou hit the water hard, swimming strongly across the river, but many were bunched up, trying to escape the torches. They splashed and fell, trying to get away. The first animal to come close to the men was speared through the lungs, not by throwing the weapon, but with just a quick, deep jab. Then the hunter pulled out the spear and looked for another target.

The hunt carried on for several minutes, animals bellowing in pain and rage. The last of them swam across the river, leaving behind several animals floundering in the red, blood-stained water. The hunt had ended. Men waded in waist-deep cold water, delivering last death blows to their prey using stone war clubs.

It was dark and in that darkness, the clan gathered together and built a fire. They had been successful in their hunt and the young children and women would live. A clan on the very edge of starvation had saved themselves, doing what many generations of cave dwellers had done.

Leather thongs were tied to the animals to keep them from floating away in the current. Altogether the clan pulled in unison, attempting to get one out of the water. They grunted and pulled and eventually one was dragged up on the river bank. Now came the women's work, the skinning, butchering and drying all of this meat.

Tonight, by the light of campfire and moon, it was time to feast. The liver was eaten raw and warm and a large piece of hindquarter was cut free using the newly made flint knives. The meat was hung above the flames to cook. Little was said, but each clan member ate as much as he or she could hold. Women chewed food for the younger ones and mouth to hungry mouth, gave them their first meat in a long time.

Daylight found the clan awakening to see many animals laying dead. Altogether they had killed seven big caribou. The cool weather of spring would keep the meat from spoiling until it could be dried. The work went on from daylight to dark for many days. Their good fortune would insure their survival.

A young child nearly two seasons of age played with a long leg bone, laughing as he walked from one person to another. This was a time of plenty and all were in high spirits.

Near the edge of the clearing, a large animal sat mostly concealed, salivating at the smells coming from the camp. He thought to just rush in and kill them all, but still he bore the scars of his last encounter with this most dangerous of foes. He would wait until dark and then sneak in silently and take a large piece for himself.

Daylight was fading to dark and when he could no longer stand the hunger pains, the great bear strode into the middle of the camp, heading toward the meat. A cry went up from a child, alerting the entire camp. Just as he was about to close his great mouth onto a large piece, he felt the sting of a man's spear as it entered his chest behind his front leg. Then it was many men, all coming at him. He roared loudly in pain and tried to escape, but their spears struck him several times, making him angry and weak. He made a short run at a man and broke his back with one swipe of his great paw. Then more spears stung him and with his last bit of fury, he killed another man.

His strength faded and deep inside his great chest, the heart that made him so powerful ceased beating and became still. He had lost his last battle. Now his flesh would nourish his enemy and his great coat of long dark fur would keep them warm. If he were to die, this was the way it should happen, quickly and taking some of his enemy with him. Now and forever, he would feel no hunger.

The clansman who had been killed by the great bear lay silent, unmoving. As was the tradition of these people, they scraped a deep hole in the earth and arranged his body so that he sat upright with his spear in his hand, ready for his next battle. Then the soil was once again put in the hole, a small bit at a time by all the clan. When the body was all covered, they placed many rocks over him to keep the animals from digging his body up. He would fight again in the next world.

The man with the broken back lived until the sun rose high in the sky the next day. He too was buried in the same manner.

Work went on in this hunting camp for several more days. As soon as the last of the meat was prepared and stored in hides, they made preparations to leave this area. These men were nomads and traveled the vast reaches of Minnesota and Canada searching for a place to call home for a season. They followed the great rivers and made camps as they went, staying at some places for several days.

On one unusually warm evening, they decided to make camp close to a small river. Here there was a large open area free of the insects that usually plagued them. There was a shelter formed from a large slab of granite rock in case it rained. They built a fire and sat near it, talking back and forth deep into the night. The leader lifted his head to look at the sky and saw under this granite ledge evidence that men had built fire here before. Smoke from untold fires had blackened the underside of the great rock. Many peoples over the years had used this place and many in the future would do so as well.

Down the river a short distance, a loon lifted its pointed bill to the sky and spoke to Gitche Manitou of his joy, his complete happiness to be back on the Bigfork River for a season.

Chapter 1: Flower

In northern Minnesota there's a place where all rivers, great and small, are forced to choose between a course that takes them toward the warm waters of the Gulf of Mexico and the frigid waters of Hudson's Bay and eventually the Arctic Ocean. This place is called the Continental Divide.

This is a place of unequaled beauty, a place untouched by the rough hands of man. This is a world so freshly formed that the handprints of Gitche Manitou, if one looks closely, can still be seen in His handiwork.

Choosing a southward course takes the water into the warmer areas of our world where lush green plants grow and many Indian cultures live on its shores. Taking a northward course means hard rapids and many waterfalls. The water runs fast and free, tumbling and churning over many miles, with very few people to see it. This course is of such beauty that Gitche Manitou only allows a few men to go there, and these have to be as tough as this land and willing to face the great Bigfork River on its own terms.

Wil Morgan was such a man, tried and tested by that great river and not found to be lacking in any area. He was a young man raised hard and lean with coal black eyes and a quick smile that flashed like diamonds. He wore a wide brimmed hat and his large hands were calloused from his labor. His beard, mostly black, was neatly trimmed with some gray starting to show through. His constant companions were a big yellow dog named Jake and a Colt .45 revolver.

Minnesota in the early part of the century was a wild place full of danger and adventure. Wil spent most of his early years trying to make a living from the land. He was a trapper, a hunter and a lumberjack, but more importantly a jack of all trades. Wil was a free man and traveled the countryside much the same way that a herd of caribou migrates to find better grazing. When game was scarce, he moved to better hunting grounds.

One unusually hot summer day Wil stopped into the Waskish Indian camp on the Bigfork River to see his long-time friend Sam Three Toes. They had been children together and hunted anything they could get close to. He pulled the canoe up on the bank and Sam came down to see him.

"And what brings my good friend Wil to our camp?"

They reached to grasp hands and kneeled down on the grass facing each other.

"Well, Sam, I heard that a little girl fell into the river about fifteen miles up from here and the people of the village can't find her. I'm pretty sure she drowned, but just the same I gotta look around for a while," said Wil.

"I can help you look, my friend, but the river moves fast now and a child wouldn't make it very far in this current."

"You're right, Sam." Wil looked down at the grass.

"Come in for a while and rest, Wil. My woman will make fry bread for you."

"That'll be great, my friend. I could eat a skunk right about now," Wil responded, and the men both laughed.

As the friends walked uphill to his lodge, little children from the village recognized him and ran to see him. Sam's oldest boy Gray Duck was nearly ten summers and one of Wil's favorites They would sit for hours telling stories back and forth. Wil had grown to love that boy as if he were one of his own.

He rolled on the ground with them in a play fight, laughing and tickling the children. Then he rolled over on his back like a vanquished foe, and they all jumped on him once again. The children were all round-faced and healthy looking. He was a welcome friend and the children all liked him.

Wil walked into the lodge and then went over and hugged his old friend Fawn. She was somewhat embarrassed and motioned for him to sit at the table. Her smile showed many missing teeth, not unlike the smiles of most women her age. There was little in the way of medical care for the Indian population. She made them a good meal and watched them eat. Then Wil told her about the little girl. Fawn was a good woman and had given Sam several children.

"Are you staying with us tonight, Wil?" asked Fawn, smiling.

"No. I better keep looking for that little girl."

She gave a slight frown and looked over at her husband.

"Maybe Wil thinks that I'm getting too old to warm his blankets," she said, smiling.

Wil grinned at her.

It was the custom of many Anishinaabe men to share a wife with a good friend, and Wil had been there several times over the years.

Wil ate his meal and then walked down to his canoe leading a dozen laughing children.

"You come and see us again soon when you can stay for a few weeks. It's been a long time since we hunted together," said Sam.

"I'll do that, my friend, and maybe your woman can put some fat on these skinny ribs."

They laughed as Wil pushed the birch canoe out into the current, pulling hard on his paddle. The current was strong and he looked for signs in the movement of the water indicating where the paddling might be a bit easier and his progress somewhat faster. The going was slow at best because of some yet unseen storm many miles away that was bringing the mighty Bigfork to life. Usually at this time of year the river moved slowly, but now it was rushing and surging toward the great sea many hundreds of miles away, the same way it did in the spring time.

The day was wearing on to late evening and Wil had found a wide part of the river where the current wasn't quite so hard. The sunset was coloring the sky with deep shades of reds and blues. The reds usually meant that there was a fire somewhere, perhaps many hundreds of miles to the west. He pulled the canoe close to the river bank and stepped out onto the rocks. His legs were sore from being in one position for so long. He stretched mightily and looked around for a place to make camp.

One of the first things he noticed was the large number of songbirds sitting in the trees and shrubs nearby. Two hummingbirds came close to his face, making a loud whirring sound. He grinned at how bold they seemed for their small size.

This spot was one where he had trapped in winter, but had never seen in the middle of summer. It was beautiful with tall walls behind and a small spot that was sheltered from the rain by an overhanging slab of granite, an excellent place to build a fire. He walked around for a while both upstream and down to get a feel for where he was. Then he went to work gathering some firewood and in a short time had plenty for the night. The heat from the fire felt good to him.

Wil pulled his canoe up near the fire and unrolled his

blankets. The evening sky had darkened and the only light around for many miles came from his fire. As the sparks rose upwards, he followed them with his eyes for a moment and noticed a darkening on the rocks above him. This place had been used before as a shelter and he wondered if it had been used by his friends or people from hundreds or even thousands of years ago. There was no way of knowing.

It was still and warm but this little place seemed sheltered from the mosquitoes. He sat at the fire for a long time, thinking about his friend Sam and his family. Wil had a lot of friends, but it seemed that he didn't get to see them often.

He rummaged through his pack and found a small can of beans. This sounded like a pretty good supper to him. Fawn had sent him some fry bread so with all that, he had a meal fit for a king. Such simple things were to his liking.

As he sat slowly enjoying his meal, he noticed several yards away a small balsam tree with a large number of lightning bugs decorating its branches. It seemed a bit early for things like Christmas trees. He chuckled softly with no one to hear. The whole place felt quite special, like he was where he should be on this night. He knew deep inside that God guided his steps, taking him on a course that sometimes allowed him to help others. Now he wondered silently what lay in his path.

He looked over at a small log and grabbed it for a pillow. He wrapped it with a blanket and lay his head on it to test it for comfort. It was just high enough to give his neck something better than laying on the ground. He took a deep breath and let it out slowly. Wil was in his element. This was his home, the land he loved. The sparks from the fire climbed slowly into the darkness and faded. In a very short time, he was asleep.

Somewhere on into the small hours of the night, Wil awoke to the sound of someone walking softly on the rocky shore. He didn't move or even breathe. There were men around who would kill for anything, bad men who robbed and murdered for any kind of gain. His hand went to his Colt .45 slowly, very slowly. Its cold feel in his hand gave him a large degree of comfort.

The intruder moved closer, a step at a time, hardly making any sound at all. Then, when he was sure that the interloper was close enough, Wil raised the Colt and cocked the hammer, all in one fluid motion.

"You're almost a dead man. This gun is quite able to take your head right off at the shoulder. Now, grab some of that small wood by your foot and throw it on the fire," said Wil with a steady voice.

The little fire crackled and grew slowly to where he could almost see. Then a small flickering flame erupted and cast its light upon the face of a young girl, barely sixteen years old. She was shaking from fear or cold and Wil wasn't sure which. He placed the gun back in its holster.

"What's your name?" Wil asked.

The little girl didn't answer.

"What's your name, girl?" he asked a bit louder.

A small voice came to life.

"Flower."

"I'm Wil Morgan."

She was shaking badly and it looked as if she hadn't seen food for a very long time. She wore a plain buckskin shirt and old blue jeans. She wore no shoes or moccasins and her hair was long and tied behind her head. Her face wasn't that of the Anishinaabe, but of some other tribe he didn't know. She had a longer, heart-shaped face with eyes larger and lighter than he had seen before. Her height nearly matched that of Wil and that surprised him some. She was still shaking, but the fire was continuing to grow and soon she was warmed thoroughly. Wil gave her a blanket to put on her shoulders.

"Where ya from?" asked Wil.

The girl wouldn't answer. She just looked off into the darkness.

"Where are your people?"

She still stared, not making a sound.

"That's alright. Some people don't like to talk much. Are ya hungry?"

Flower looked him straight in the eye and nodded.

"I haven't eaten anything but berries for three days. I am very hungry."

The fact that she hadn't eaten for three days made him think. This might just be the girl who had fallen into the river three days ago.

"I'll cook ya some bacon and fry bread."

The girl nodded and smiled at him. She was unusually pretty and her smile revealed perfectly white teeth.

Wil had the frying pan heating up and some cold fry bread was heating on a rock. He threw in several pieces of bacon and chopped up a small potato. Flower looked interested in what he was doing. She looked at him once again and then with a soft push, moved Wil away from the fire so she could do the cooking. Wil sat on a stump watching her. By the way it looked, she had done this before.

Wil looked down river and it was just starting to get light. Some small birds were awakening along the river and the morning show was about to begin. The sun was casting its first fiery rays on the granite rock they were camped by and it showed streaks that sparkled in the sun. Then from nearby, a chorus of red-winged blackbirds started to sing. He looked over at Flower and it appeared that she too was enjoying the show. They shared a quick smile.

By the time the food was done, it was daylight and they sat eating in silence. Flower looked up once in a while, grinning as she ate. Even though she hadn't eaten in such a long time, she still ate one mouthful at a time, slowly.

Wil thought for awhile of what he should do now. Her people would be looking for her. Still, he wondered where she had come from. She didn't look like the rest of them. He knew that sometimes women and children were taken by raiding parties and used as slaves. This could be what had happened.

"Where is your family?" asked Wil.

Still Flower wouldn't talk. She walked down to the river and washed the frying pan and plates with gravel.

"Do you have any soap?" she asked.

"Got some lye soap. That alright?"

Wil fished into his pack and found a large bar of brown soap and threw it to her. Then she turned to washing herself up. Her hair was long and was the first to get attention, then her face and arms. She waded into the river and took off the rest of her clothes. She washed thoroughly, even scrubbing her buckskin shirt and blue jeans. Wil was watching her and in a few moments their eyes met and Flower motioned for Wil to go back to the fire.

"Can you give me a blanket or something to cover up with?" asked Flower.

Wil grabbed a blanket and hung it on a branch near the river.

"Thanks, Wil Morgan."

Flower walked up to the fire and hung her wet clothes near it to dry. She seemed to be in a bit better condition, now that she was fed and had the chance to clean up some. Wil tried not to stare at her, but she was the prettiest Indian woman he had ever seen.

"Do you feel like talking yet?" asked Wil.

"I guess I'd better talk now since I ate most of your food and used up your soap."

"Oh, that's alright. I've been looking for a child who fell into the river upstream from here quite a ways. Could that be you?"

"I guess that might be me, but I'm no child and I didn't fall into the river. I jumped."

Her English had none of the French Canadian accent that he was so used to. She seemed to be from a far distant place.

"Tell me all you know, Flower. I need the whole story."

She looked at Wil, trying to decide if he was someone she could trust. If she made a bad choice, she'd be in a worse condition than before. She said nothing for a few moments. Then she made her decision.

"I'm not going back."

Wil was somewhat surprised by her strong voice.

"Those people stole me and my brother Little Bear from my home a long time ago when I was very small. A raiding party came to our camp and killed all our men. They took many women and children. If they tried to fight, they were killed. Most went quietly, hoping that they would be rescued. The first night on the way here, my mother tried to rescue us. They caught her and killed her in front of us all. I remember how we cried over her dead body.

"They gave us no food for a long time and my brother nearly died. He was a year older than me. We stayed on that trail for many days until we came to the river not far from here. The old women beat us and made us work hard all day. My brother grew stronger as he got older, but he still got many beatings.

"As I became a woman, many of the men wanted me for a wife. I refused to lay with them so they beat me more and more. Then my brother told me that he was going to travel north and get away from these bad people. He said that he was going to follow the river until he was far away. I know my tribe is all dead now except for us two and I want to find my brother."

Wil sat quietly, letting Flower tell the whole story. It seemed to him that she had a lot to say that had been kept inside for a long time.

"If those people thought I had drowned, I would have a better chance of getting away. So in the morning, when all the people were outside, I walked into the river and it took me downstream. I could hear the men yelling. I took a deep breath and put my head under the water. When I came up, I was far from the camp. I did that many times until I got very tired. Then I swam to the river bank and started walking. For a few days, I ate berries and nothing else.

"One day I heard some men calling my name, but I hid up in a tree for many hours until they left. I was very scared. I thought they would kill me or beat me some more. Then I started to travel just at night, hoping I could get far from those people.

"At night, as I was moving along in the moonlight, I smelled a campfire and food cooking. I walked very quietly so I wouldn't be caught. Then a man said something about shooting my head off."

Wil grinned at her.

"You know, Flower, you just can't be too careful. This is dangerous country."

Wil laughed a bit and Flower too seemed to be a bit more at ease.

"What are you going to do with me?" asked Flower.

She had somewhat of a defiant look in her eyes.

"I'm not going to do anything with you. You're a free woman and can do as you please. I'm glad that you told me all this, but I don't think that there's much chance of you finding your brother, though. He's probably a long way from here by now."

Flower's clothes were now completely dried in the summer sun. She walked behind a large rock and got dressed again. When she came out, Wil was once again quite surprised at how pretty she was. She was still barefooted, but that seemed not to bother her. Wil had a small piece of buckskin in his pack and asked her if it was enough for a pair of moccasins. She went right to work cutting them out.

"Can you help me find my brother?" asked Flower.

"I don't know about that. I have hunting and trapping to do and have to be ready when winter comes. I might head downstream for now, but I gotta keep busy trying to make a living. This is a tough country, and if I don't keep working, I'll starve this winter."

"I can paddle a canoe, shoot, cook, trap, tan hides and damned sure take care of myself. I won't be any trouble to you. If you're heading downstream, that's where I want to go anyway." She grinned. "And I can fatten you up some too."

Wil laughed loudly, throwing up his hands. It seemed that he had himself a partner, quite possibly the prettiest partner any river rat could ever imagine.

They spent the day just resting. Flower seemed like she was pretty tired and not quite ready for the rigors of paddling a canoe all day. Around noon Wil looked up and found that Flower was gone. She had said nothing, but disappeared as quietly as she had come. This left him wondering what had happened. He thought that he might just get the canoe loaded and head downstream as he had originally intended, but then he changed his mind. He walked to the river bank and got a pot of water to make some coffee. Still he wondered about Flower. His thoughts ranged back and forth from her to trapping to hunting to home, but they always returned to Flower.

His coffee was bubbling away now, making a hissing sound as it boiled over onto the fire. The sun was hot and beating down hard on his head. It was unusual for him to be just resting. It wasn't his nature. The coffee was starting to smell pretty good and within just a few minutes, he had a steaming cup in front of him. He thought to treat himself by adding a small amount of sugar, but that was something he rarely used because of its high price. He waited for it to cool some and drank it slowly, enjoying its strong flavor.

Around mid-afternoon, he found a shaded spot and quickly fell asleep.

Flower was slowly making her way through a large grove of balsam trees, looking for their next meal

A time later when he had gotten all the sleep he needed he started to awaken, drenched in sweat from the summer sun. What greeted him was the smell of roasting grouse. He looked over toward the fire and there was Flower looking back at him. She had killed three nice grouse and had them cooking on sticks near the fire. As he watched she would turn them each a little at a time, making sure that they didn't burn.

"Now where in the world did you get those?" asked Wil.

"Well, I learned a long time ago that if you want to eat, you better learn to feed yourself. I killed them with stones."

"How many of those can you eat?"

"I already ate today. These are for you," said Flower.

"You're quite a hunter and a good cook as well, but I can't possibly eat even two of them, so I guess we'll have to eat them together. They'll spoil if we try to save them."

Wil was right. No meat lasted long in that heat. It had to be consumed while hot or it would make you badly ill. Flower knew this too but was trying to show Wil how useful she could be. She needed to find her brother, but now as the last rays of the evening sun lit her face, she couldn't think of anyone else that she'd rather be with. She thought Wil was the most handsome man she had ever seen.

The evening campfire was always a time to share thoughts and tell tales. Flower had never seen much other than the years of hard labor by her captors. Wil told her about trapping and hunting trips. Flower wanted to know how old he was and if he had married. Did he have children and parents nearby? She was a good listener, but more than that, Wil appreciated the chance to hear a woman's voice, something of a rarity for him.

The campfire was finally allowed to die and Wil unrolled his bedroll. He stretched out fully and yawned. He rolled to his side, facing the fire. She thought about blankets and saw that there were no extras. Flower crawled over to him and lay down alongside him. She pulled the blankets over them and snuggled closely. She was a very pretty girl and in some respects, an innocent child that he would need to protect.

＿＿＿　＿＿　＿＿＿

Much further downstream and to the northeast, Little Bear sat watching a large cow moose and her calf cross the river near his camp. He knew enough about nature not to bother a moose when she had a calf. It was a great way to get killed and he wasn't ready to meet his maker quite yet.

His camp was made this night on a small spot of rock that ran out into the river. There was no brush growing nearby and even the slightest breeze kept the mosquitoes away from him. Someday he would make his lodge and he hoped that it would be in a place with a breeze.

He had gone many miles on foot since leaving the camp of his captors. He had waited until his sixteenth summer to make his second attempt at escape. It was a hard trail, but not like when he was ten. Now he was strong and could run for many miles without stopping.

He found what was left of a busted up birch bark canoe and was able to repair it. Now he would be able to cover many more miles in a day.

He thought of his sister and wondered if she would be all right. There was no family for her and that would make her life harder. Little Bear thought back to the way he was treated years ago at the hands of his captors. He was forced to work hard all day without food and nearly died of hunger. When he was no longer able to work, they beat him some more. One older woman took great pleasure in seeing him cry.

On an unusually hot summer day, he was made to work in the sun digging for roots. This was always woman's work and they hated doing it. He had been given something to eat in the morning but near noon he was in need of food and water. His stomach was tied in knots and he sat on the ground and cried. At nine summers he was tough, but he was still a small boy deep inside. The old woman saw him sitting alone, crying, and she grabbed a stick with the intention of beating him again. He saw her coming and tried to get away. They had tied his leg with a buckskin thong and he wasn't able to escape her wrath. The old woman raised the stick over his head and it came crashing down across his back, sending a fine mist of blood into the air.

His fear turned to rage and from somewhere deep inside, he gathered the courage to withstand the beating, standing tall and defiant, not making a sound. This provoked the woman and she beat him some more, determined to make him cry out in pain. After being hit nearly a dozen times, blood running down his back, he turned and faced his tormentor, taking the weapon from her hand.

"No longer will I let you beat me. Today is the end of this torment you have put me through."

He broke the stick in half and handed the pieces to the old woman.

His life in the camp of his captors eventually got better and he wasn't made to work without food. He was still an outsider and a slave, but at least he was fed.

In the summer of his tenth year, he was determined to escape and go back to where he had come from. He thought that there might at least be some of his tribe left, some of his relatives.

Summer was a time to gather berries and put away food for the winter. He put aside his own supply of food, trying to get enough saved to last him on the long trail home. He had pemmican and dried meat and a large supply of fresh berries to eat along his trail.

The time had at last arrived to make his escape. His supplies were hidden near the village and in the middle of a very dark night, he slipped outside and quietly made his way into the woods. There was no moonlight and he tripped and fell several times in the dark. He found his hidden supplies and started the journey southward, to what might remain of his people.

He put the small pack on his back and started to run, staying on the open game trails. At nearly 4:30 in the morning, the sky was turning light and he was able to see a bit better. He trotted along making good time, putting several miles between himself and his captors. By mid-morning, he had covered several miles, taking a course that led him upstream along the Bigfork River. He stopped for a while to eat and drink some water. His heart was racing and it was uncertain if it was from exhaustion or fear of being overtaken while he rested. He eventually caught his breath and ate some ripe raspberries, their sugar sweet flavor giving him a burst of energy.

As he rested, he heard the rustling of the tall grasses behind him and bent forward so as not to be seen. The sound became louder and then a large timber wolf came running by him only a few feet away. The wolf was intent on his own trail. Little Bear's heart was again racing but the faintest of smiles grew into a large grin. He had survived a close call with one of the forest's most dangerous predators.

By mid-afternoon, he was many miles from the camp and he slowed his pace some. As he walked along, it came to him that he was free, free to go where he wanted when he wanted to. This was a new feeling for him. He was free.

He stopped for the night by the river, and made a small fire to warm himself. He had supplies that would last him for several days, but he didn't want to waste them. This was a long trail that he had started and he didn't want to run out of food before he found his people.

Morning found him cold and shivering. He needed to warm himself and decided to start the day by running. As he moved through the pines and alder brush, his thoughts returned to the camp of his captors. He tried hard to understand the way they thought. Little Bear was a slave and some tribes used many of them and even traded for them with other bands. He had value and he was sure they'd be after him. He kept up a fast pace.

Near noon, he came to a place where the ground was soft and decided to cross the river to make better time. This also might keep them from reading his trail. He was a young boy but was starting to think like an adult. He walked into the water and swam across. He sat down in the sun to dry himself, his thoughts running like a fast river. When they came looking for him, they would see that he had to cross the river to keep from going into the swamp. He thought of maybe crossing the river several times and even swimming for a while just to confuse his trail. His thoughts were maturing, and he was no longer a child aimlessly fleeing from his enemy. He would use his head and it might just save him. He was sure they knew his general direction of travel, heading back to his people. He had to change his course or he would be captured again, or worse, killed.

His trail the next day led him westward. He crossed two small rivers and then came to some open country that was mostly just tall grass. Eventually he came to a great lake and camped near the water, the breeze keeping the mosquitoes away from him and allowing some much-needed rest. He thought that he might be over halfway back to his people.

He saw a large bird sitting on the ground near a small tree and picked up a rock. His arm came back slowly and the rock flew true to its mark. The grouse fluttered around in the grass and he ran to claim his prize. His meal was cooked over a small fire and it was difficult to wait until the bird was done. He sat back on a small log waiting for the bird to cook. His thoughts wandered for a time and he tried to remember his mother. Her face had started to fade from his memory. He remembered how she used to take care of him, making his clothes and teaching him about the foods of the woods. He thought of his uncle who took him fishing and his aunt who used to make him fry bread. Those were good times for a young boy.

"Is there enough meat to share with a hungry old man?"

Little Bear nearly fell backwards off his log and then looked the old man right in the eye. He definitely didn't recognize him.

"Who are you?"

"I am Black Feather, Chief of the Red Lake Band. And who are you, small warrior?"

"I am Little Bear."

"I think that maybe you are far from home. Where are your people?"

"They are hunting not far from here, and will be here soon," said Little Bear.

He was doing his best to look brave in the face of such an important man.

"I will share my meat with you, my brother."

The two sat and ate in silence, neither making an attempt at conversation. Soon the bird was gone and the man belched politely, throwing the used-up carcass into the flames.

"You cook well for one so young. Where does your trail lead you?" asked the man.

"We are hunting near here and my people will return soon."

"You are far too young to be on the hunt. Tell me the truth, little warrior."

Little Bear looked the man straight in the eye once more and couldn't find any reason to fear him.

"I am trying to find my way home to my people. I was taken by some bad men several years ago and they killed my mother. Now I have escaped and am searching for my family."

"Tell me where they live."

"It seems so long ago. We lived in a place where two great rivers come together many miles south of here. There were many people in my village. My sister and I were the only ones left alive."

"I think I know your people. Are you Sioux?"

"I think I am, but I'm not sure. Maybe Mandan," said Little Bear.

"That is a long trail back to your home. Do you think you can do it, little warrior?"

"Yes. The trail is burned into my mind and I have supplies to last me."

"Are those bad men looking for you?"

"I am sure that they look for me, but I keep moving every day as fast as I can. If they find me, they will take me back and I would rather be dead."

"You can come to my village. My old woman will fatten you up," he said and laughed. "We have many children in our band and you would have many friends. We do not take or keep slaves to do our work."

"No. I better move on. I have a long journey to make."

"You will make this journey, but do not forget to ask the Great Spirit for wisdom. Even at your young age, you need to seek his face," said Black Feather.

"I will do this."

That evening they slept close to the fire and sometime during the night, the bad men caught up with them. Little Bear heard a war cry and saw two arrows slice into the heart of Black Feather, killing him quickly. Little Bear got up to run off into the darkness and another arrow stuck into the back of his shoulder, knocking him to the ground. A man from the camp on the river grabbed him and dragged him back to the fire. He spun Little Bear around and pulled the arrow from his shoulder. Then he knocked him down onto the ground near the fire. It all had happened so fast. Black Feather was dead and Little Bear was bleeding badly. His trail had ended.

Little Bear's life went back to being one of hard labor. After he healed up, they kept a close eye on him, thinking that he might try to escape once again. He had learned a lot on this trail. When he tried again, he would have weapons to protect himself. He would wait until he was older and wiser. Then he would find his people.

His years on the river were hard, and his sister was being constantly chased by the men of the tribe. He protected her as much as he could, but he took many beatings for her. She was special to him and as far as he knew, she was his only relative.

Little Bear sat in the near darkness thinking. Now he had escaped again. He was older, though, and the men who chased him would find him to be a fierce opponent. He would cut the throat of any man who tried to make him captive. He was now a man and the Great Spirit had given him a large amount of courage and wisdom.

▬▬▬ ▬▬ ▬▬▬

At the village of Sam Three Toes, life went on as usual. There was hunting to be done and for the women of the village, there were hides to be tanned. Sam had been on a hunt for several days and game had been abundant. His trail led him nearly to Canada, where he and Wil had hunted many times in past years. On this hunt, he had decided to take along his son of nearly ten summers. The name given him was Gray Duck because at the time of his birth, a large gray duck had flown low near their lodge. It was most certainly a name given by the Great Spirit.

On this day they paddled slowly to the south, heading back to their village. All through the heat of summer they were forced to dry whatever meat they took, wherever they were. It made for slow going, but their birch canoe held nearly a hundred pounds of dried meat of different kinds.

Gray Duck had grown strong and was good company for Sam. Paddling a canoe all by himself made for some very long days. This year was different, though. He spent many hours teaching his son all he'd need to know when he got older. It seemed to Sam that this young one was learning fast, but the smile on his face made him wonder. Every time he looked at the boy he was grinning. It made Sam think that he might just love life.

Back at their village Gray Duck was loved by everyone. He helped any time he could and the older folks seemed to really appreciate him. He would get them fire wood or just stop in to say hello.

On this morning Sam was going to try to catch some fish and he asked his son to stay at camp and keep watch on the drying meat. The boy had done this many times and could tell when the meat was sufficiently dried, taking it off the drying racks. He was a good worker and made his father proud.

Sam got into the canoe and pushed off into the main channel, following the current downstream to where he had caught some fish the day before. He had found some big fish and speared several. As he neared the spot again, he saw in the clear water another school of big red horse. These weren't the best tasting fish, but they were easy to spear.

Sam sat still in the canoe, watching for one to come close enough to spear. He would throw the spear hard, and then pull it back to the canoe using a rawhide thong. In a couple hours, Sam had taken three nice fish.

Back at their camp, everything was quiet except for the small crackling sound of the fire. On this day, there wasn't even a breeze to keep the mosquitoes off Gray Duck. He kept the fire going hot enough that the maple brush he had sat on top would smoke quite a bit, curing the meat. When the smoke faded some, he checked the venison again and it looked like it was well cured. He took a piece of buckskin and unrolled in on the rocky ground. Then he laid the meat out to cool for a time.

He was doing his job handling the meat when he heard something crack brush off to his right, away from the river. His first thought was that his father was coming back, but when he looked up, the sound had come from the wrong direction. Then he heard it again, but closer this time. He was starting to feel a bit fearful and reached over to get his knife. If someone was going to try to harm him, he'd fight to protect himself and he'd fight hard the way his father had taught him.

He watched for quite a while in the direction he'd heard the sounds but he heard nothing more. He returned to his work, feeling more at ease.

Over in the brush, less than a hundred yards away, a big bear lay on its side licking at his back right foot. A steel trap had a good hold on him and no matter how hard he tried, he couldn't get it off his leg. The whole leg was swollen and near the jaws of the trap the leg smelled bad, making him lick at it incessantly. The pain he felt made him nearly crazy at times. He had dragged the trap around for several days. His first encounter with the trap had surprised him and he howled in rage and pain. His great strength allowed him to break the trap free from the tree that held it, but the trap still had a hard grip on him and it followed him wherever he went.

The trap now kept him from finding a meal. He was forced to stay near the river and lakes because his body needed water. His fever was raging and he was angry. From down river, he had smelled meat. He had eaten nothing now for a long time. His anger and his hunger combined now to make him into an entity that no other creature would be able to withstand.

Gray Duck was rolling up a hide when he again heard something. He looked up and saw the great bear, now standing only a few yards away, looking directly at him. He took up his bow, ready to take a shot if the bear came any closer. He looked back at the river and thought of running for it and swimming to the other side. His options were narrowing now. There was very little distance between them and the bear was shaking his head back and forth, making a popping sound with his teeth. To the bear it appeared as if the boy was challenging him just by not running away.

Sam Three Toes had taken all of the fish he wanted to for the day and put away his spear for the short trip back to their camp. It wasn't far away. As he paddled, he saw a patch of raspberries and stopped to get some lunch, some variety in his diet.

The bear, in a flurry of black roaring anger, came for Gray Duck. The boy drew his bow and an arrow went deep into the bear's chest, but it did nothing to stop his charge. In less than a full heartbeat, the bear had knocked the boy to the ground and had a grip on his neck. He shook the boy back and forth like a dog shaking a rabbit. The life had been stolen from Gray Duck and he couldn't even feel the savage mauling the bear was giving him. After a time of making certain the boy was indeed dead, the bear sat on his haunches and licked at his leg some more. A large drink from the river did little to make him feel any better. He came back to the lifeless body and stood over it, cocking his head from side to side watching for any movement. Each time he exhaled, a spray of blood flew from his great mouth and nose. The arrow had pierced one of his lungs.

The animal started to feel weak and panic arose from inside. He grabbed the lifeless body and shook it some more, venting his climbing rage. He dropped the boy once again and looked around the camp. He drank another large amount of water and then went to the lifeless body, clamping his great jaws around the boy's chest. He walked off into the woods, the trap making a bright tinkling sound with each step. In a short time, he tired and lay down next to a large pine log, resting his head on the boy's body.

Sam Three Toes was getting close to camp now and as he came around the bend in the river, he noticed that there was no smoke coming from the fire pit. He thought that to be a bit odd. He yelled to Gray Duck, but there was no answer. He paddled a bit faster and when he hit the shore, he stepped over the side of the canoe and dragged it up on shore a short distance. He walked over to the fire and saw the whole story in the tracks, the blood, and the boy's hunting bow, now laying partly burned in the fire.

It was clear that something terrible had happened and it looked as if Gray Duck had been killed by a bear. Sam took a piece of dried meat and put it in his pocket, and picked up his bow and a quiver full of arrows. He would find his son.

The trail was wide and when it crossed a sandy spot, the tracks showed the marks left by the trap on the animal's foot. He had only gone about a half mile when he saw the bear asleep near a log. He put an arrow to the string and with all his might pulled it back. The arrow sunk into the bear's chest, but there was no movement. The bear was already dead. He walked up and saw Gray Duck's body beneath the giant bear's head. The boy had been killed, but he had taken the life of the bear. He lifted its head and pulled what was left of his son clear of the animal. Then he sat on the log and cried to his maker. He saw the trap the bear had been caught in and the reason for his great rage.

The clan on the Bigfork River had once been known as the bear clan, and as such thought of the great bears as being their brothers. It had always been something he didn't fully understand, but now it was starting to make sense to him.

Sam carried the body of his son back to the camp on the river. He laid his body on some fresh buckskins and washed his face and cleaned his wounds. Tears flooded the man's eyes and he mourned out loud for his son. Gitche Manitou had need of this boy and Sam would never be able to fully understand it all.

A great stack of dry pine wood was made and what was left of the boy was gently placed on the pile. He put the boy's knife and what was left of his bow next to him. Then much more wood was added, covering him completely. His trip to the next life had begun. Sam started the fire and sat back on a log watching the flames consume his boy, his future. He kept the fire going all night and by morning, there was little left but a pile of ashes. At the next rain storm, Gray Duck's ashes would become a part of the river.

Sam loaded the canoe with all of the meat and his hunting bow. The trip back to their village would take him several days. It seemed so strange to him to be going home alone. As he paddled, it came to him that the bear had come to Gray Duck so that they could meet Gitche Manitou together. It was not his place to question the Great Spirit, but when it was his turn, he would ask why he took a young boy instead of an old man. This gave him some comfort, knowing that some day he would know all.

His return to the village was a sad time. His wife Fawn and the other children cried for several days and in the evenings they built fires and sang songs about the small boy with the big smile.

Chapter 2: Downstream

When Wil finally opened his eyes, he saw that Flower had already gotten a good fire going and had the coffee boiling. She had never made coffee before, but it looked like she learned quite well from watching him the day before. The smell of that and the bacon frying in the pan was more than he had ever expected so early in the morning. He squinted at her from through the flames and she was just as pretty as the day before. Still, he wondered what kind of trouble this would cause him.

"If you sleep all day, you will go hungry. It is a good thing that I found you or you would be starving by now." Flower's laughter was like water splashing over rocks.

Wil laughed with her and sat up, scratching his head.

"Have you been up long?"

"I awoke when your snoring scared me. You sound like an old moose in heat." She grinned.

Wil laughed hard. He'd never heard comments like that before.

"What's for breakfast?"

"Bacon and fry bread."

"That sure sounds good."

He moved close to the fire and reached for the coffee pot but she beat him to it and handed his cup to him. Then she handed him his breakfast. Wil had never been waited on before and felt a bit awkward at being treated so well. They ate quietly and when they finished, Flower got busy cleaning up the camp.

"Flower, we need to talk. Come sit down here with me," said Wil.

She came and sat by Wil, and by the look on her face, she seemed to be expecting the worst. Maybe she had burned his food or maybe the coffee was not very good. She had been in trouble many times when she was held against her will, but now it was different. She was actually trying to please this man and had apparently failed.

"We need to talk about many things, but first, you need to know that you don't wait on me. We share the chores and we take care of ourselves. You are a free woman and you make all of your own decisions."

She moved closer to him on his log. Flower smiled at Wil and seemed quite pleased with her new friend. There had been few times in her life when she was treated so kindly.

"Thank you, Wil Morgan. I'll do my share of the work and that will make life good for us both." She smiled broadly, still not able to fully comprehend her good fortune.

"We'll search for your brother Little Bear as we trap and hunt the river. We may never find him, but we will look. Today we head north on the river. I've heard that the trapping there is good, so now we'll have to find a place to spend the winter."

They sat together closely for a long time with neither

willing to break the silence. The beauty of summer was all around them and Flower was smiling. She seemed to be accepted by Wil and stood on her own merits, an equal partner. Wil indicated that he was done talking and they got the canoe ready to go. Wil always kept a spare paddle lashed to the bottom of the canoe and untied it for Flower to use. She looked at it for a moment and said that she would make a better one when she had time.

All their worldly possessions were loaded and Flower got into the front of the canoe. Wil stepped in and pushed off, letting the little birch canoe be taken away by the current. The morning was already hot and would be a lot more so by afternoon. As they paddled, Wil noticed that Flower could handle the paddle well and they made good time. Within a couple hours, they had gone quite a distance.

Flower turned to Wil and put a finger to her lips.

"It sounds like there is some bad water coming up. We should go to shore and walk to it," said Flower.

"No. It can't be that bad. We can handle it."

Flower got a serious look on her face and turned back to her work, paddling in time with Wil. She thought that the sound of the rapids was growing a bit faster than she liked. Then she saw what it was that made so much noise. It was a long straight stretch of white water with a lot of large scattered boulders. She turned to Wil and saw that he was grinning. Still they paddled into the middle of the river, into the mouth of the beast, and the little canoe bounced lightly over the water. Her heart was beating hard and she was doing her best to keep up with Wil. She was intently studying the boulders and current and in just a short time, they broke free of the rapids. She turned to look at Wil and he was laughing at her. She had a very serious look on her face. When she turned back to keep paddling, Wil hit the water hard with his paddle, throwing a spray of water all over her back. She turned quickly to face her attacker and gave him a dose of his own medicine.

"Wil, you are a crazy man. We should have portaged around that place," she said in her most serious voice.

"If we would have, we'd still be back there getting the canoe ready. I've been here before and it isn't that bad. Maybe next time we come here we can portage, while we look for strawberries." Wil grinned broadly.

He dipped his paddle again into the water and they went on downstream. They continued paddling hard for quite a while, both tiring out in the heat. The extreme heat of the summer was wearing on them and both needed to rest.

"Do you need to cool off for awhile?" asked Wil.

"I sure do. It's very hot today."

"Let's head to shore and find a spot to swim."

They paddled toward shore and Flower grabbed a low hanging branch to stop the canoe. Wil was out of the canoe in a moment and they pulled it up on the shore a short way. The air was calm and the deer flies were chewing them up quite badly. Wil sat on the ground and took off his boots and shirt. He unbuckled his belt and removed his revolver. He emptied his pockets and ran down the bank, diving headfirst into the water. It was cool and even more importantly, he got some relief from the flies.

"You look that way," said Flower, pointing across the river.

Wil looked away and Flower quickly took off her jeans and buckskin shirt. Then with a short run she too jumped into the river. The cool water made them feel extremely invigorated and ready to finish the day's paddling. After a few minutes, they were both dressed again and laying on the bank, drying off in the sun.

"Did you ever go to a school?" asked Flower.

"No. We lived a long way from a school, many miles. My folks tried to teach me, but I fought them off."

They both laughed.

"Actually, my mother had been a teacher a long time

before I was born so they took my education pretty darned seriously. I had to study each day after the morning chores were done. My mother did most of the teaching, and my father taught me about numbers."

"That sounds wonderful. I learned some numbers and a few different things from Mah Tee, one of the elders. I heard them talk about a great ocean and a place where it never snows," said Flower.

"I have seen the great ocean to the east, the Atlantic, but I have never been to the Pacific ocean out west."

"You mean that there are two of them?"

Wil laughed. "There are several oceans, and some day before I get too old, I'd like to see them all. My father was the captain of a great ship that sailed all over the world. He told me of things that I probably will never see. He said that in some places, people kill and eat men. He said that some men are black and some are yellow, but I have never seen such a thing."

Flower sat still with her eyes open wide.

"One time many years ago, the company that he worked for told him to sail to a place called Africa and bring the cargo to where the Mississippi River empties into the ocean. He sailed for several weeks and when he got there he dropped anchor a half a mile off the coastline. They readied a small boat called a dingy and four seamen rowed him to shore to meet the traders. He wasn't quite ready for all he saw.

"The man he met and was to do business with was nearly drunk and a half empty rum bottle sat on his small wooden desk. It appeared that the man hadn't bathed in an awful long time. Sweat stains ran down the back of his filthy shirt.

"The man shook the captain's hand and asked if he was ready to load his cargo. They walked down a long catwalk and into a warehouse, and the further he went, the darker it got. Then he heard a scream and something made a dull thud in a room close by. The captain looked at his short-term companion and the drunk just grinned at him. Then he heard another scream and turned to go into a small room where the sound had come from.

"There was a small lantern hanging in the middle of the room and over in the corner was another man in the process of raping a young black girl barely twelve years old. The captain grabbed the man by the shoulder and spun him around. As he faced the man he swung his fist hard, knocking him to the floor. The rapist scrambled to his feet to face his attacker and saw that it was the captain who had hit him. The fight went out of him in an instant and the small girl ran back to what he figured was her mother.

"In a very short time, the whole scene unfolded in front of him. The man dealt in slaves. He had a large cargo of black men and women chained to the floor and walls of this small room and it stunk badly. This was the cargo he was supposed to bring back and he flatly refused, walking at a quick pace to the boat and the waiting crew.

"Black men from many different tribes, captured men and women from other tribes—they sold them as slaves to any men who would buy them. My father was a good man and refused to accept a cargo of men and women all chained together like animals.

"He knew that he would be fired for not carrying out their orders so he sailed to the Dutch West Indies and bought a load of spices and silk. When he returned to port, the owners were waiting for him. His refusal to take on a human cargo got him dismissed as captain, but another company hired him the very next day."

"Is it the same thing as me being held captive and made to work?" asked Flower.

"It is the very same thing."

Flower thought in silence for a very long time, tears gathering in her eyes.

"Are you ready, Wil? The river waits for us."

Wil groaned and sat up.

"This is the prettiest place I've ever seen," he said.

"Where I come from we have many rivers, but they all go south to where it gets hot. I like the cool nights here much better."

"Have you ever built a cabin?" asked Wil, getting to his feet.

"I have helped build many lodges, but not a cabin. That would be much nicer."

Wil grinned. "We'll have to start a cabin in a week or so if we're going to get it done for the winter."

Wil lifted the canoe to the water and once again they started to paddle. The water seemed to be slowing down some. Whatever it was that caused the great Bigfork to come to life had passed and the water was back to the way it usually was in summer, flowing slowly and steadily.

For a time Flower kept quiet, thinking of all that Wil had told her in the past hour. She too had been taken as a slave. She too had been taken from her mother. She too had been raped and used badly by many men. If her life were to continue the way it was she would have killed herself, but it now seemed to her that the course of her life had changed. She would do her work each day and if Wil decided to use her or rape her she would endure it for a time, hoping to find her brother. Deep inside, though, she thought that Wil was a good man and would never hurt her.

Flower paddled with a smooth rhythm that Wil found easy to match. They covered several miles without any conversation and by late afternoon were many miles from where she had first found Wil.

When Wil spoke, it jolted her back to reality. She had been lost in her thoughts for several minutes.

"Our supplies are starting to run a bit low so we'd better get to a trading post soon. We'll need flour, salt, sugar and a few more things to get us through to spring. I know there is one down a few more miles, but I'm worried that there might be people there looking for you."

"You said that I am a free woman. No man can ever take me again." She sounded like she was willing to fight for her freedom now.

Wil kept paddling and seemed to be somewhat concerned about the kind of men that hung around the trading post. He wanted no trouble, but always faced it head on when he had to. The day was wearing down toward evening and he decided to pull in at the next good place they found.

"Let's see if we can catch a few fish for supper, Wil. I have some small string and a couple hooks."

She caught a small frog and put it on the hook. It swam out into the river, trying to get away from the one who had put him on the hook. It had only gone a short distance when the water near it churned and the frog disappeared. The fight was on. The great fish was bent on getting away but was faced with the determination of a young lady who wanted to cook him for supper. The two pulled in different directions for quite some time until the fish tired and was hauled, hand over hand, to shore. As it got near the bank, Wil grabbed it and threw it up on the shore. He let out a loud whoop and went to admire Flower's catch.

"Now that's what I call a fish! Walleyes are the best tasting fish on the river. I've fished for a long time and never even seen a fish like that!" said Wil.

Flower didn't say anything, but she seemed to be pretty happy with her contribution to supper. Wil took out his knife and proceeded to clean it up. Flower already had the frying pan near the fire and had a piece of bacon cooking for the grease. Wil dusted the pieces of fish with flour and threw them into the pan. Then they added some salt and pepper for good measure. They were both quite hungry, since it had been a long time since breakfast. Wil found a couple blue steel plates and sat waiting until the fish was sufficiently cooked.

Flower put several large pieces on their plates, and while the next pan full of fish cooked, the feast began. They both ate a lot of fish and it seemed to Flower that Wil had a system to eating it without swallowing the bones. He would put the fish into one side of his mouth and a steady stream of bones came out the other. He salted his fish liberally.

"It shouldn't be too much further until we get to the trading post now," said Wil. "If we hurry, we can be there by noon tomorrow."

"I have never been to a trading post," said Flower. "What do you do there?"

"Well, I suspect that you can buy anything that you have enough money for."

She looked perplexed at the term "money." Wil thought for a moment and realized that she had been held captive for a long time and had never even thought about buying anything. She had had a hard life and all of this was new to her.

Again that night they talked for a long time, trying to learn all there was about each other. They were becoming close friends considering they had known each other for such a very short time. Wil saw her through different eyes than he had when they met. She was no longer a cold and wet child, but a woman, a much prettier woman than he had ever seen before. She seemed to stand tall and proud and had an air of confidence.

The sun was a large, deep red orb, smoldering silently like the embers in a fire. As it sank closer to the trees along the river bank, it seemed that those same trees should catch fire and burn. A large gray duck flew low across the river and directly into the face of the sun. For just a moment Wil watched to see if the bird would be consumed even though he knew it could not happen. The river this evening was silent as if waiting for something to happen. Of such things came the magic of this river, the Bigfork River.

The fire was allowed to die down and the beginning sounds of nighttime on the river made them aware that they weren't the only creatures there. The sky was again full of sparkling stars and in time the northern lights started to blaze brightly downstream to the north. They swung and gyrated back and forth, sometimes nearly going all the way to the ground. The colors were almost hypnotic, going from nearly red to blue and white. Sometimes the colors were so brilliant that they could almost hear them.

"Will we go to where the great lights are?" asked Flower in a small voice.

"No. That's way too far for man to travel. That's where the Great Spirit lives," said Wil, smiling.

Flower was still thinking about Wil's father.

"Did your father sail those big ships for a long time?"

"No. He worked on the ships as a young man and as he grew, he went to the Naval Academy to learn all about sailing. It was like a very large school."

"Where was that?"

"Out near the Atlantic ocean, I think. Way off to the east. He was made a captain in five years and then sailed on the big ships all over the world.

"One time he told me about a voyage he made to a place called China. He was supposed to get a load of silk for the ship's owners. That's a very light cloth and the thread is spun by little silk worms. While he was there, a man asked him to take a load of boxes to a place called Macao and he would pay cash for his services. My father took the cargo and his crew put it into the hold for the trip. The transaction would net the boat's owners nearly two hundred dollars.

Their ship the *Free Trader* sailed on the tide near midnight. They set a course to Macao and were under full sail making good time. On the third day, the watch called out that there was a smaller boat under sail overtaking them on the port side. My father didn't think too much about it for a while, but the small ship was gaining on them. He told the boatswain's mate to call general quarters and the ship came alive. Their ship the *Free Trader* had no cannons so if she was to be boarded, he could do little to stop it.

When the small ship came within a hundred yards it fired a shot across his bow, signaling him to stop and be boarded. He had little else he could do and called for the crew to haul in the sails. The smaller ship stayed a distance off and it appeared that there were several canons aimed at him. Then a small boat was lowered and rowed up alongside. The man who boarded first carried a small pistol and his crew carried rifles.

My father asked him what he wanted and was told to produce the ship's manifest. The pirate was obviously an oriental man. He had the entire crew lined up along the railing and one man kept a rifle aimed at them, waiting for his orders.

What the man wanted was the cargo my father had picked up and was delivering to Macao. They brought it up on deck and one of the pirates was told to open the first crate. Inside the first box was silk, but upon closer inspection, there was opium rolled up in the silk cloth. Altogether there were nearly a hundred boxes and the pirates took it all, not bothering with anything else on the ship.

This was my father's first encounter with pirates and opium, and for the rest of his career he did his best to stay away from both."

"What is opium?" asked Flower.

"It is a brown powder that men smoke. It makes them see strange visions."

"Is it like ergot?"

"Yes. The same thing that grows around here."

"I have seen what it does to men and it scares me," said Flower.

The camp was quiet with only the sounds of the fire

crackling once in a while. Wil had once again made his bed by the fire and found something on which to lay his head. In the nearly complete darkness, Flower came to Wil and lay close to him. He shared his blanket with her again and they lay quietly listening to the soft rhythmic sounds of the Bigfork river as it flowed to the north. She felt very warm next to him and his thoughts turned to the fact that she was a woman. It had been a very long time since he had a woman so close to him. He wanted her badly, but he wouldn't take advantage of one so young. She snuggled closely, their legs touching, their arms entwined.

And so they passed the night, each wanting the other, each having a hard time sleeping.

Morning was something different on this day. It seemed that there was a bit more laughing and breakfast was eaten in near record time. The canoe was brought to the river bank and everything was again loaded. Before the sun had come up completely, they had already gone a couple miles.

"Tell me once more about the trading post."

"It's like a large cabin with many things inside. They have many kinds of food to eat and blankets for the coldest winter. There are guns and ammunition and candy."

"What is candy?"

"It's sweet like maple syrup, but in many flavors and colors."

"Candy," she said, rolling the word softly on her tongue, and kept paddling.

In the short time since she had met Wil Morgan, he had given her many things to think about. The fact that the world was so large made her feel small and insignificant.

It was getting closer to noon and off in the distance, they saw a small wisp of smoke. As they got closer, it was apparent that it was the place they had been looking for. It kept getting closer and the level of excitement in Flower's voice grew considerably. They came around the last bend in the river and saw the long awaited trading post. There seemed to be people nearly everywhere. When they found a good spot, they pulled the small canoe up on the bank and covered their cargo from prying eyes. Then they walked together toward the store.

Inside, the place was dimly lit with only a few small windows and a few coal oil lamps. The smell was musty and the dirt floor seemed littered with small pieces of trash. It was, in general, quite a mess, but the goods seemed to be in acceptable condition. Wil had a fair amount of cash saved from his years on the river and he looked carefully at the price of each item. There were many men inside, all looking over the goods.

"Take your squaw outside. We don't let no Indians in here," said a gruff-voiced man in a green plaid shirt.

Wil looked at the man and decided to just ignore him. He might have been speaking to any of the other men there.

The clerk walked up closer to Wil so there was no mistaking who he was talking to.

"Are ya deef?" asked the man.

Wil moved up next to him and when he was so close he could smell the man's foul breath, he as quick as lightning grabbed the man by the throat.

"I'm not deaf and Flower will stay here with me while I buy what we need. Now, do you understand?"

The man was visibly shaken and seemed to want no part of Wil's temper or his fists. He let go of the man and dusted off his vest, stepping back. Flower was over in a far corner doing her best not to be seen.

"How much for these blankets?" asked Wil.

"Four dollars," said the clerk.

"Now where in the hell did you get that price?" yelled Wil.

"Alright. Alright. How about two dollars?"

And with that, Wil and the clerk got to some serious bargaining. There were dry goods like flour and salt, leather goods, potatoes, coffee and bacon and a few more traps. Wil walked over to Flower and took her by the hand, showing her all of the things that were in the store. She was most interested in items like colored ribbons and the large jars of peppermint candies. Wil helped her pick out a pair of shoes but Flower didn't like the way they felt. She got socks and a good coat and even some canned peaches, which she had never even heard of before.

"How much you give me for that birchbark canoe of mine? It's the third one from the end."

The clerk went to the door and looked out at the canoe on the river bank.

"I'll give you six dollars and if you buy a new one, I'll give you seven."

"How much for a new cedar and canvas one?" asked Wil.

"Sixteen dollars."

"Let me see it."

They walked into a dimly lit back room and the clerk lit another lamp. He pulled a couple blankets from over it and Wil turned it over.

"I'll take it if it don't leak."

"It ain't gonna leak," said the man.

Then Wil walked back into the store and found Flower looking at new jeans. He held them up to her and, allowing some room for growth, picked out a one-dollar pair. He opened up a big jar and told the clerk he wanted a pound of licorice and one of peppermint candy. Wil had a model 94 Winchester and figured that it was good enough for anything he'd have to shoot so he didn't need much but another box of shells.

"I guess that'll do us. What's the damages?" asked Wil.

"Well, that comes to $21.20 and for cash money, I'll throw in an axe."

"And a couple pickles?"

"And a couple pickles." He grinned.

"Done," said Wil. "Flower, go get us a couple of those big dill pickles."

She smiled at him and walked to the back of the room where the barrels were. She pulled out two large ones and looked them over. They had a sour and salty flavor, unlike anything she had ever tasted. She took a small bite and it made her eyes pop open wide.

Wil reached into his pocket and pulled out a small roll of bills. The clerk watched carefully, and it seemed that his eyes grew wide upon seeing his money. There weren't many people who had cash money in these hard times.

"Are ya buyin' fur next spring?" asked Wil.

"I am, but it's gotta be good fur. I pay cash money and I can do some better if'n we trade."

Wil was satisfied with his purchases and said that he'd be back. As he walked toward his canoe carrying some of his purchases, a man with a long beard and white hair stopped him.

"You been in this area for a long time?" he asked.

Wil just kept walking. "Yup."

"You been down south?"

"Some," said Wil.

"How's the trapping?"

This was nearly unheard of. No man asked about another's trapping. Those things were kept quite secret. Wil knew that he was new to the area but he didn't want to be friends with such a man.

"You wanna team up for the winter?" the stranger asked.

"Already got a partner."

"I'm a good trapper and a fair cook too."

"Don't matter. I don't need another partner."

The man walked away muttering under his breath about shooting somebody.

"What did you say, old man?" asked Wil quite loudly.

There were several men around and all had stopped to

listen to Wil shouting. The old man had stopped walking, his back turned to Wil.

"You got something to say old man, spit it out," said Wil.

The man started to walk again and Wil figured that it was all over. He turned back to his work, unloading the canoe. The man turned toward Wil again but this time he had a handful of gun. They were only about twenty-five feet apart, but the man's aim was bad and the shot whizzed past Wil's ear. Wil Morgan fell to the ground reaching for his Colt .45, but before he could aim, there was a soft sound like someone hitting a drum and a knife was sticking from the man's chest, right near his heart. His eyes were open wide as he sunk slowly to the ground.

Flower had been walking toward the canoe and saw the whole thing as it played out. She was only about ten feet from the man, and when he drew his gun, Flower pulled out her knife. Her aim was true, but way too slow. If the man had been a bit better of a shot, she would have been paddling the new canoe alone.

Wil walked over to where the man lay on the ground. His eyes were open wide, staring blankly into the cloudless sky. A few of the other trappers gathered around and looked down at the dead man. He had been a thief and an opportunist. Any man who came near him was in danger of his quick temper. Two old-timers names Sven and Ole came up to Flower and patted her on the back. Minnesota's Arrowhead region had just been rid of an awfully bad man.

The man who ran the trading post came walking up to the crowd.

"Anybody know this guy?" he asked.

"He's a bum and a killer," said old Sven.

They rolled him on his side and checked his pockets for money or some form of identification. They found a grand total of two dollars. The clerk said he'd bury the man for that amount and that was the end of that. He had opened his mouth to cause trouble and died right there on the river bank. They all figured that the world was a much better place without him.

They got the new canoe loaded and hefted the paddles that came with it. There was even a spare paddle lashed to the floor just as Wil had always done. This canoe was seventeen feet long and not nearly as nimble as the birch canoes he had used for years. It was heavy, but with all their cargo, it was necessary. Wil and Flower paddled out into the main current and were carried downstream, quickly putting the trading post in the distance.

Little Bear sat on the river bank, trying to determine where he was. The river led him in a new direction, away from where he had lived as a child. He had fashioned a bow and several arrows. The canoe he had found was now in good condition and kept out the water of the river. He missed his sister Flower and wondered if she would ever be able to get away from her captors. She was the only blood relative left in his world. He still carried a fading picture of his mother deep within his heart. She had been ruthlessly killed at the same time the boy was taken.

He had a small fire going and was roasting a muskrat he had arrowed earlier in the day. His meals had been lacking in variety, but they gave him strength to paddle further and further each day, getting away from his captors. He was young and lacked experience, but he made up for it with his youthful enthusiasm. As he sat there on the bank of the Bigfork, he tried to decide what his goal was. Was it just escape or did he want to start a new life on the river where he could spend a lifetime? He didn't want to be alone, but for now, it was necessary.

Daylight was fading and he turned to his small fire and the meal that awaited him. It was meager fare, but he had seen many days where his captors had completely refused to feed him. The muskrat was fat and he rubbed that fat on his body as a way to keep himself warm. He gathered small reeds and grasses, making a blanket for the coming night.

He lay close beside the fire watching the embers fade to red and gray dust. He turned his face upward to the night sky.

"Gitche Manitou, have mercy on this man."

Chapter 3: Jake and Charles

Wil and Flower didn't much like the way the clerk had treated them, or the way he had looked at Wil's money, and they wanted to put as much distance between them as possible. Any time that there were dealings concerning money, Wil expected something bad to happen. He always said that money brought out the worst in men and he was rarely wrong about that. Then there was the dead man who had tried to shoot Wil. If the old man had friends, they just might want a bit of payback.

As they paddled the Bigfork, they were used to hearing nothing but the water and the wind. Anything else was reason to be on the alert. For the last three days, they had been hearing an occasional cracking of brush along the river bank but were never able to see what it was that made the sound.

"Are you about ready to make camp? There's only about another half hour 'til it's dark," said Wil.

"I'm pretty tired too," said Flower. "We've been paddling hard for several days now."

With that, Wil headed to the next opening they saw on the bank and started to unload the canoe for the night. Flower got busy right away gathering wood and making a fire. With them both being so tired, a meal of beans and biscuits seemed to be in order. Flower had taken over most of the cooking, mainly because she feared that Wil's food might kill her. That always made for a good laugh for him since he'd lived to this ripe old age cooking most of his own meals.

As they sat there in the near darkness eating their supper, Wil once again heard something crack brush near them. He drew his .45 and aimed it at where the sound had come from. After a few minutes, Wil put the gun away and relaxed some. Flower was a bit nervous since she'd never seen Wil draw his gun so fast. They finished their meal and went to pull the canoe a little closer to the fire. The supplies were near the river bank, but Wil didn't think they would get wet even if the river rose some in the night.

"Did you have any friends when you were a boy?" asked Flower.

"Ya. There were a few families on the river, but it was a long way from our place. One was named Wilbur Withers. He was from out near the Atlantic ocean, a long way from here. Whenever he started to misbehave, his father would send him to spend the summer with me."

"Was he a bad man?"

"No. He just liked excitement."

"What did you do in the summer?" asked Flower.

"We hunted and fished and paddled this river from one end to the other over the years. One time we paddled north for several days and ran out of food. Wilbur had a rifle with him and we needed to shoot a deer or starve. Our plan was for him to sit in front of the canoe and shoot any deer he could see.

"We had just come around a bend in the river when he saw a big bull moose in the water not far from us. He raised the gun to shoot and when the smoke started to clear, the big animal was almost on us. I jumped over the side and at the same time the moose hit the canoe, tearing it to pieces. Wilbur swam for the other side of the river and I was right behind him. We got to the shore and turned to see the moose still doing battle with the canoe, but by that time there wasn't much left of it. He bellowed loudly each time he saw a bit of canoe and kicked it into small pieces.

"It seemed like he had been at it for a long time, and then just as quickly as he had started, the moose stopped and then walked back to shore. Just as he stepped on dry ground, he tipped over and lay dead. We had found our food, but in the process had lost our canoe and rifle.

"We cooked up some big steaks and tried to dry some of the meat for the long trip home. As we sat by the fire that evening, we tried to figure where we were. By canoe it was a long journey home, but on foot it was a terrible distance. We were nearly into Canada.

"The next morning Wilbur waded around in the river looking for his rifle. The bottom was all rock and within just a short while, he found what he was looking for and held it up high. He had a smile on his face nearly a yard across. Now we stood a good chance of making it home.

"We dried a lot of meat that day and made a backpack out of birch bark and moose hide. The next day we awoke to find all the rest of the moose meat had spoiled and we were left with just what we had dried. A pack of nearly a half dozen wolves found the smell of the meat too much to resist and did their best to take it from us. We figured it was time to head home.

"We walked along the Bigfork river for many days. Each evening we'd make a fire and eat some of the meat. The weather was turning colder and we had to keep a fire going all night. At the end of nearly a dozen days on the river without a canoe, we walked into our cabin. Dad didn't hardly look up from his writing. Ma seemed glad to see us and cooked us some pancakes. That sure did taste good. We'd had some fun before on the river, but that one turned out to be quite an adventure."

"How old were you then?"

"I think we must have been fifteen."

"Quite young for such things, weren't you?"

"Ya, I suppose we were, but we grew up quick," said Wil.

"You're lucky that moose didn't kill you," said Flower, shaking her finger at him.

"I suppose," he said with a grin.

Wil was starting to look a bit tired and yawned several times. He rolled out the blankets, but this time, Flower didn't lay down right away. She sat watching the sparks from the fire drift skyward, into the face of the creator. Her new friend lay asleep only a few feet from her and soon he was snoring. The sky was brightly lit from stars and a full moon sitting just above the maple trees. Then she saw something that gave her a moment of fear. There near the river, just on the other side of the pile of supplies, was a wolf. She could see his head just sticking up from behind the pile, looking at her. His head would go down and then in a moment it would come back up, keeping an eye on her.

Slowly, while his head was down, she would move her arm closer to the rifle. She watched closely and moved only while his head was down. As her hand touched the cold metal, she grasped it firmly, lifting it to her shoulder. Then she could feel the steel butt plate come in contact with her bare shoulder and she settled the rifle in snugly for a shot. Her right thumb pulled back on the hammer and with a soft click, it was ready to fire. The big wolf raised his head once more in the darkness and then the small campsite on the Bigfork River lit up brightly, but just for a moment. Wil immediately rolled several feet away from the fire and came up with his .45 cocked and ready for action. Flower picked up a couple pieces of small wood and threw them on the coals.

"What in the hell was that?"

"We had a wolf trying to steal our supplies," said Flower. "I think he's all done stealing now, though. I shot him in the head."

Wil walked over to the fire and took a burning stick to use as a torch. As he walked to the river bank, he heard something move and once more raised his Colt .45, ready to finish it off. His burning torch showed an animal, laying still but looking up at him. It was bleeding badly from the head and didn't seem able to move. It had the look of a domestic pet, but he'd seen wolves of most colors and sizes before. It was all yellow from head to tail. Then it moved again, but this time it was trying to wag its tail in friendship. Wil bent down to touch it, and it made an attempt to lick his hand. This was a dog, a dog unlike anything he'd seen in a long time. It appeared to be a full grown Labrador retriever. Flower had the fire built up brightly by then and he was able to see it more clearly. This was what had been following them along the river for so long. It looked to be nearly starved. Flower was there looking at where the bullet had creased his head and brought some grease to put on it. The dog whimpered some but didn't move to get away. They decided to leave it there for the night and see if it was still there in the morning.

They both agreed that a dog would be a good companion, but it wasn't theirs and someone would be looking for it. If it stayed for a while, they would name it. The fire faded and they wrapped up in their new blankets for the night. Flower still preferred to lay close to Wil.

At first light, Wil was awake and getting the coffee going. The yellow dog was still there where they left it and Wil seemed afraid to look over there to see if it was alive. He threw some bacon into the pan and watched it dance around as if trying to find a comfortable place to cook. Then he looked around for a potato. As he was searching in his pack, the dog came up behind him and licked his neck. Wil nearly fell into the fire from surprise. He figured that not many critters licked their victims before they ate so he was a little safe, anyway. The dog had survived the night and was ready for something to eat. He wagged his tail so hard that it sounded like a war drum beating on the ground.

Wil grinned and reached over to pet the animal. He tried to think of something to feed the dog, but he wasn't going to give up any of his winter supplies. As he sat thinking, a small beaver surfaced across the river. Wil reached for the rifle and neatly, with a single shot, killed the animal. There was a rush of yellow and the big dog flew through the air with a great leap and landed nearly a third of the way across the river, swimming strongly toward his breakfast. When he got close enough, he grabbed the beaver by its back and turned to bring it to Wil. As he reached shore, he stopped for a bit and shook the water off his back and then dragged it by the fire. He sat by Wil's leg, as if to ask what he wanted done next.

Wil took the beaver and removed the pelt, throwing the hind quarters on a rock near the fire to cook. The dog would have a good meal.

Flower finally got up and walked over to Wil, putting her arm around his waist.

"I was watching you and the dog. He is a good one for sure, Wil Morgan."

"If nobody comes looking for him, we keep him."

They ate their breakfast and loaded the canoe for another day's paddling into the furthest parts of Minnesota. The countryside was spectacular and the river smooth. The big dog sat on top of the load, keeping an eye open for game. Whenever they would jump a duck, he would get excited and look back at Wil, waiting for him to shoot.

Evening once again found them in a part of Minnesota that

Gitche Manitou must have reserved especially for them. There were tall pines all around them and a small stream entered the mighty Bigfork, adding its water to the great river. The water from the stream was nearly clear when put into the coffee pot. Wil dipped his hand into the water and took a taste of it. It was sweet, unlike the brownish water of the great river. That evening as it was getting dark, Wil made a mental note of this place. He wanted to follow it back to where it came from. Other men came up and down the Bigfork and silently he wondered if anyone else had ever seen this place.

The next morning as the sun started to peek above the trees, Wil once again scooped up some water from the small creek for his morning coffee. He turned back toward the fire and as he walked, he glanced once more at the water. A glint of gold mixed momentarily with a ray of sunshine and revealed itself to Wil. His heart raced for a time and then slowed again.

"Flower. Come over here."

She walked up to him and seemed a bit perplexed by the look on his face.

"Did you just swallow a frog?" she asked, grinning.

"Look inside the pot."

She looked closely, turning the container back and forth.

"It sure looks like gold, Flower."

"I have seen it many times before," she said.

Wil walked back over to the stream and bent down to take another scoop of water and gravel. The dog waded right in and with his front feet, tried to help Wil with whatever he was doing. Wil poured it all into a steel dinner plate and rocked it back and forth, watching closely for the familiar glint of gold. There it was again. Small flecks of gold were mixed in with the sand. This had the makings of being quite interesting.

"I know we should stay and pan for gold, Flower, but if we do, we'll never survive the winter. We have to push on and maybe we can come back again in the spring. For now, though, we have to hide this place."

Flower seemed somewhat surprised by the way Wil was acting. She had seen this before when she was held as a slave, but nobody ever gave it a second look. Wil cut some brush and tried to hide the small stream. This had the makings of real wealth for them, something most men would never see.

When their work was done to his satisfaction, they sat and drank the rest of their coffee.

"Why did you cover that stream? I know where there are a lot of streams like this and all of them have little bits of the yellow stone."

Wil seemed incredulous. "You mean that you know where there is more gold?"

"Yes. I have seen it many times."

Wil had a large clump of thoughts coursing through his mind and each and every one of them contained the riches of gold. If Flower could indeed guide him to more gold, they might just be rich some day.

They loaded the big canoe and once again were paddling in the sunshine, heading for somewhere, not caring much where the river took them, the big yellow dog watching their every move.

Evening found them camped near a small rapids. The only flat place to build a fire was uphill about twenty yards. The canoe was safely tied to a rock just in case the water level rose during the night.

Their camp this night gave them a spectacular view of a large lake nearby. It appeared to be no more than a quarter mile away. They decided to spend a bit of time exploring it and in the morning they would walk over to it.

Dinner was once again a bit easier than usual. Flower fried up some pancakes and dusted them liberally with cinnamon sugar. The treat was wonderful and raised their spirits. Wil figured that if they ate like that all the time, he'd gain a few needed pounds.

As they sat by the fire watching the sunset, Flower seemed to be a bit more quiet than usual.

"Is something bothering you?" Wil asked.

"Not really. I was just thinking what it must be like to live with Gitche Manitou. Sometimes I am afraid to die and at other times, I'm not."

"I'm in no hurry."

"I'm not either, but when I see a sunset like this, it makes me wonder what is on the other side," said Flower.

"I'm still in no hurry."

They sat quietly watching the last rays of the sun disappear behind a far hill. The sky had been so red that it looked like it was on fire. Now it had faded and all that remained were the stars. That too was spectacular.

After a while, Wil unrolled his blankets and found a comfortable place in the green grass, not far from the fire, to sleep. The night breeze was warm, keeping the small insects from discovering them. Wil lay on his side watching the last small flames of the fire flicker and die. Flower came to him and lay down on his blankets. Her leg covered his and she reached over to touch his face in the darkness. Wil put his arm around her and pulled her close, the warmth of her body rising.

Morning found Flower again with little to say. She cooked some potatoes and bacon for their breakfast, handing a plate to Wil.

"You are a good cook, Flower," said Wil.

Still she had little to say. Then she set her plate on a rock and went over to Wil, kneeling in front of him. She took his half-eaten plate of food and set it on a small log.

"I have something to say to you, Wil Morgan. I am not a little girl. I am a woman."

Then she stood again and handed Wil his plate. They finished their meal with no more conversation.

The portage to the lake was short and it appeared to be worth the lost time. The water of this lake was nearly as clear as glass. They got into the canoe and paddled toward a small island. Even in deep water, they could see fish on the bottom. The early morning sunshine gave a gold appearance to the water's surface. In a short while they came to the island and got out to look around. The dog got out first and ran around, getting some exercise. The place was covered by huge pine trees with little brush. As they walked on, they came to a fire pit, long since abandoned. There were two steel posts and a steel crosspiece. Nearby they found a steel pot, and a couple rusted forks. It looked like someone had forgotten this place a long time ago. There was little else to see and they decided to just leave things as they were.

After another hour paddling around the lake, they decided to go back to where they had started from and get back onto the river. They had lost a few hours, but they both were glad to have seen such a nice lake. Flower was asked if she wanted to name the lake and decided to call it Ice Lake because it was so clear.

After a couple more days, Wil decided that the new member of their party would get a name. There was no ceremony or pronouncement of a name, he just started to call the big dog Jake. Flower seemed to like it quite well and used the name too. And so it was done. Jake became a part of their group and as such, was given chores to do. Wil taught him to fetch sticks for the fire and he did it with relish, trying his best to please his master. All he wanted in return was a pat on the head once in a while, not much pay for such loyalty. On hot days, Wil would have him fetch sticks thrown into the river. He made the big dog wait until he was told to fetch and it seemed hard for this enthusiastic retriever to do so. Then when the word was given, he would run for the river bank and take a great leap, sending a spray of water several feet ahead of him. The dog seemed to be around three years old and once he started to fill out from good food, he was quite large. Sometimes in the evenings when they were just watching the fire, Jake would leave camp and go hunting for himself, but he was always back when it was time to move on.

Wil and Flower had a fondness for raspberries and if there were some nearby, they were always included in their meal. One late afternoon they spotted a large patch of berries and decided to make camp for the night. After the wood supply was gathered and the canoe dragged up on the bank, they decided to go and get some.

The heat from the sun was doubly hot in the raspberry patch. There were so many berries that they ate nearly as many as they put in their bucket. Wil smiled at Flower and saw that she already had a red coloring on her lips. This was one of summer's finest rewards.

They were only a few feet apart when Wil heard a sound and saw the plants wiggle just a short distance from him. He looked down at his feet and saw a small bear cub nearly sitting on his foot. This was trouble for sure and Wil spoke softly to Flower.

"There is a small cub right next to my foot and it looks like a she-bear between us," said Wil, whispering.

Flower started to back out of the berry patch and Wil followed closely, keeping an eye on where the sow was. They had just cleared the raspberry patch heading for their camp and both started to run. There was a low growl and Flower looked up in time to see the bear right behind Wil. She was growling loudly and made a quick grab with her front paws, trying to trip Wil. Her claws just caught Wil's pants and sent him rolling with the bear nearly on him. Then there was a flash of yellow as Jake joined the bear in battle. He was snarling loudly and nipping at the bear, but more importantly he was keeping it from killing Wil. The big dog kept the bear's attention and that gave Flower time to go and get the rifle. Wil was right behind her and grabbed the 30-30 from her hand. The bear was still locked in battle with Jake, but by the time he got near enough to shoot the bear, both she and the cub had climbed a tree to get away from Jake. He aimed the gun at the bear's neck and was pulling softly on the trigger. The big bear was just doing what bears do when they have cubs. He decided to leave the area to the bear.

Wil and Flower paddled another couple hours until they found a spot of land that ran out into the river, completely devoid of trees and shrubs. Normally this time of year, the mosquitoes ate anyone they could find, but with a slight breeze they were blown away. This little spot was ideal and would give them a good night's rest.

Wil stepped out of the canoe and steadied it for Flower. Within just a few minutes, she had a fire going and a meal in the works. Wil had gathered more firewood and unloaded the canoe.

"Tonight will you tell me about your mother?" asked Flower.

"What do you want to know?"

"Everything."

"That's a mighty tall order. She was a complicated woman."

"Everything."

Wil laughed and went back to gathering firewood.

Jake had eaten his nightly roasted muskrat and now lay close to the fire, nearly burning his fur. He looked like he was almost asleep already. Wil unrolled his blankets a short way from the fire and lay back with his head on a small log. Then Flower smiled at him and lay down also, but with her head on his belly, a much more comfortable pillow. The night was still and the sky once again full of stars. Off on a hill not far away, an old timber wolf hailed the rising moon, making lesser critters think of places to hide. Jake trembled a bit at the sound.

"Tell me of your mother, Wil."

Wil took a deep breath and held it for a while. Then he exhaled and started to speak of a woman he loved very dearly.

"My mother was born in Belgium and went to school in Paris. She was a trained musician and singer and she could shoot quite well too. She met my father while he was a captain of a sailing ship. They married and he then left her in Paris for five months while he sailed to America and then Australia. She taught school while he was gone.

"My father had only been gone for a few weeks when mother noticed that she became sick each morning, so she went to see a doctor. He gave her the good news that she was pregnant."

"Was it you?" asked Flower.

"Yup. It was me alright. Father came home to find his wife very pregnant. They talked for quite a while about all of the things they wanted for their child and between them they decided to move to Minnesota. They homesteaded some land and built a log home. My father farmed and trapped and did most anything to support his family.

"The years passed and the first thing I can remember is mother trying to teach me to write. I must have been a poor student because I sure spent a lot of time at the kitchen table. Then one day my father was called to St. Paul, Minnesota, on business. He left my mother and me at the cabin on the river for just a few days."

Wil stopped talking for a bit and Flower looked up to see his eyes filled with tears.

"I remember one night there was a knock on the door and my mother opened it to see two men. They asked to see my father and she said that he was off on business. That was all they needed to hear. They rushed in and took over our home. I remember trying to fight them off but I was way too small. They hurt my mother very badly. In the morning they tied her up and put her into the canoe. The only thing that I remember was they said she'd fetch a high price in the slave market up north. Slavery was a big business back then and many families lost their children."

"Why didn't they take you?" asked Flower.

"Guess I was too young to make the journey. They left me sitting at the kitchen table and I never saw my mother alive again.

"My father came home the same day and from what he told me, I was still sitting at the table waiting for someone to rescue me and find my mother. To this day, whenever I hear about slavers, I feel such rage that I could kill."

"What did your father do?" asked Flower.

"He said that he brought me to the neighbors and then left looking for her. He caught up with her captors and during the fight, they killed her by cutting her throat and my father killed one of them. The other got away. So today, I carry around a large sack of hatred, but it's only for one man. If I ever see him again, I think I might still know him, but it has been quite a few years."

Flower lay still for a long time and then she heard Wil's breathing change. He was asleep. She moved alongside him and covered them both with two blankets.

The hot days of summer were turning to fall and Wil knew there wasn't much time left to build their cabin. The cattails were turning brown and large flocks of red-winged blackbirds flew over the ripening wild rice. The year's crop of young ducks were already flying and Wil was getting to the time where he had to make a decision as to where their cabin would be.

One morning they were paddling up a small stream looking for a place to build and as they came around a curve in the river, Wil saw a cabin on the bank that looked like it hadn't been used for a long time. A small birch tree had fallen against the roof and was in the process of rotting away. They paddled up near it and Wil yelled to see if there was anyone around. There was no answer.

They pulled the canoe up and walked to the cabin. Wil yelled again but still there was no answer. He knocked on the door and then just walked in. The sight that greeted him was nearly unbelievable. The cabin was made into three rooms and there was a table in the middle of the kitchen. On the table was a plate filled with what looked like dried beans and a piece of dry bread. There were curtains on the window that now looked like just shredded cloth. It appeared as if someone just left the place before dinner, several years ago. Neither one of them said anything. There was a small metal box on the table and when opened they saw a bundle of letters, tied neatly with string. The name Charles Masters was written across each one, but the strange part was that none had been opened and none had a return address.

On the wall above the fireplace hung a picture of a family, most likely that of the previous occupant.

"What do you think happened?" asked Flower.

"It looks to me like he just up and left here a few years ago and never came back."

Wil walked over and opened one of the doors. Inside there was a straw bed and there, all covered with blankets, were the remains of Charles Masters, now nothing more that bones and shredded clothes. He had died several years ago. They walked back outside and sat on the steps to discuss what they had just seen.

"We gotta bury old Charles," said Wil.

"It looks like he got sick and just went to bed and died, all alone."

"I think we might just spend the winter here, Flower. It's a good cabin and with some cleaning it'll be alright. It's far enough from the main river where I doubt anyone would ever see us. The trapping should be good too. Do you think you could make a home for us?"

Flower grinned. "I don't think old Charles would mind, especially if I cleaned this place up some."

With that small bit of conversation, new owners took residence of this little cabin in the woods of Minnesota's

Arrowhead region. They dug a deep grave for Charles and then burned his bed and most of the cloth items that hung around the cabin. Flower found an old chest in a small room and inside were a set of curtains and some men's clothes. There was only one window in the cabin and she hung the curtains up to make it look nice.

The cabin had a sink inside to wash the dishes and the water ran from there to the outside and down to the river. There was a large fireplace and a steel cookstove that was pretty rusted up. In the back room, Flower found an unopened bottle of whiskey and some pretty dishes. There was nearly anything she could ask for.

Outside, Wil looked inside a small shed and found several dozen Victor traps hanging on the wall and a few small tools. As far as he could tell, the man was a trapper and made good money at it. Wil walked back inside and sat down at the table. After cleaning out a couple of bird nests, Flower made a fire in the fireplace and the little cabin started to look like a home. He picked up the bundle of letters. It looked like the man had died at least three years before by the postmarks on the letters. They were all addressed to: Charles Masters, General Delivery, Crow Station, Minnesota.

Flower was busy cleaning up and sweeping out the years of dust and cobwebs. She had found two oil lamps and another small steel box, which she brought to Wil. The box was rusted shut and Wil thought to just leave it, but then he thought that it might shed some light on the whole situation. He took out his knife and pried it open. Inside, the contents were still in good condition. The first thing was a recipe for white cake and one for pancakes. Under that was a small pile of money. He counted it and found it to be nearly a hundred dollars, quite probably the man's entire fortune. This was indeed a great sum of money and Wil wasn't sure how to handle it. He put the whole thing back into the steel box and set it on the fireplace mantle.

It was getting on toward mid-afternoon and Wil was moving their supplies to the cabin. This was where they would spend the winter. They would trap and hunt and try to earn a living from this land he now claimed. Flower still wanted to find Little Bear, but for now, they had to stay for the winter. Wil dragged the canoe up on the shore and tipped it over. He stood looking out over the river. He was many miles from the Bigfork River and there was little chance that anyone would bother them or their trap lines. The colors of fall were starting to change the countryside into an array of reds and yellows and the sky was turning a darker shade of blue. The water was changing too, turning dark and at times almost black. Wil had found a shotgun hanging over the doorway and there were several boxes of shells for it too. He and Jake would try to take a lot of ducks to be used in the winter.

Wil was satisfied with his new situation and felt that it would make their winter a lot easier. This land was never actually owned by anyone. You just used it to suit yourself and left it for the next man when you were done with it. This time, one man's misfortune had turned out to be another's fortune.

When Wil walked into the cabin this time, he smelled food cooking on the stove and looked over to see Flower wearing a new shirt they had bought at the post. She was a stunning beauty and Wil was always amazed at the things she could do. She could make good meals even when there wasn't much to cook. All in all, they made a good pair.

"You sure do look pretty, Flower."

She walked up to him and put her arms around his neck. Then she kissed him on the cheek, making him blush. Her long dark hair fell softly on her shoulders. She snuggled into his shoulder and kissed him again. He looked deeply into her eyes and saw the reflection of his growing love for her. Then he put his arm around her and pulled her closer.

That evening after the supper dishes were done, they sat

on the floor near the fireplace talking. Wil had decided to open the box full of letters. Inside there was a neatly tied stack of nearly thirty. They were all arranged by the date they were postmarked. He took out his knife and slit open the very first one that Charles had received, and read it aloud.

July 24, 1908

Dear Charles,

I hope this letter finds you well. Your father and I wish for you to succeed in your new endeavor. We were wrong about you leaving your job at his bank. Father has instructed me to send you twenty dollars each month from our family account and since there are no banks in your area, we will send cash. Father also says that he is sorry he said you were stupid for giving up such a good career.

Your sister Sandra is getting married next year and we hope that you can come to the wedding. She is engaged to Frederick Dunham, a student from college. He is a nice young man.

We send our love,
Mother and Father

Wil found the enclosed twenty-dollar bill and went on to open the next in the series. It too contained a twenty-dollar bill. There was a total of six hundred and twenty dollars in twenty-dollar bills in those letters and old Charles hadn't opened any of them. Not a single one had a return address. Wil had never lacked for money, but he had had to work hard for every cent he had. Now sitting in a neat pile in front of them was a stack of money like few men in these parts had ever seen. He would take good care of it in case someone came to claim it.

The next day, Wil fashioned a wooden box for the money. Inside that box was a quart Mason jar with a zinc lid holding the letters and money. Then they dug a hole behind the cabin and hid the fortune from anyone that would come looking. Wil didn't think anyone would ever come here from Charles' family, but if they did, the money would be there safe and sound.

Little Bear was steadily making progress downstream, heading northward. His canoe was light and he felt himself getting stronger as the days went on. He would try to catch fish or something else the river would provide each day. The year's berry crop was coming to an end and he would need to spend time gathering wild rice soon.

His clothes were tattered and torn and his moccasins needed to be thrown away and new ones made. Altogether he looked to be a wretched orphan with nobody to take care of him.

One evening as he sat near his fire, he smelled something new. It was the smell of meat cooking on a smokey fire. Then it was gone again and he didn't know where it had come from. He sat thinking, many things running through his mind. Should he flee from this area or maybe look around to see if other men lived nearby? This was a serious situation for him. He had few weapons to fight with but if he ran away, he might miss a chance to find a new home.

The next morning, he continued downstream slowly. He had only been paddling for a short time when he looked up and straight into the eyes of a young girl getting water from the river. He stared at her and she ran away, back into the trees. He decided to make his stand and nervously pulled the canoe up on the shore. Just as he was starting into the woods, three men came walking toward him at a fast pace. When they saw him they all smiled, giving Little Bear a moment of relief. One of the older men spoke to him and raised his arm to wave.

"*Boozhoo*," said the first man in greeting.

He had found friends and they spoke a language he knew. These were the Anishinaabe and they were good people. They invited him to their camp and shared their food with him. Little Bear had turned into a handsome man and the young women watched him closely. The Holy Man gave him a place to stay in his lodge for the night and invited him to live with them.

For his first night at his new home, he told of how he had been stolen and made to work as a slave. He told of his sister Flower and how she was planning to escape too at her first opportunity. The Holy Man told everyone that he was now a member of their clan if he wanted to stay.

His first days there, he built his own lodge and started to make some new clothing. Some of the older women helped him with the stitching. One of the younger girls named White Owl cut his hair and braided it for him. She giggled a lot, but Little Bear didn't seem to mind. He thought of his new situation and was happy to have found friends.

After he had gotten settled in, he started to hunt for the clan. He would always bring home deer, rabbit or some other meat for his people. He was good with his bow and took a large bull moose that took a few days for the people to process for the winter.

Each evening as the people gathered around the fire, he noticed that White Owl would move up close to him. She was only in her teens but made it clear that she liked Little Bear. He saw her as only a friend, nothing more, and didn't want to offend her parents.

Life had turned good for Little Bear.

Chapter 4: Harvest the Land

Fall was rapidly approaching and there was still much to be done at the new cabin. There was almost no firewood and the season to put up meat was upon them.

Nearly every morning, Wil would set out five or six decoys and take as many ducks as they could clean for the day. He sat partially concealed on the shore waiting for them to come in and Jake would let him know when it was time to shoot. He'd make a soft whining sound and Wil would look to see where they were.

"Steady, Jake. Now let's not get in a hurry, boy."

And then the 12 gauge would explode and a duck would splash into the water. Wil would quickly reload and sometimes if there was still one within the range of the gun, he'd shoot again. The two made a good team with Jake knowing what was expected of him. Wil would then stand

and Jake would sit close to Wil's left leg, waiting to be told what to do. It was quite a sight. The animal quivered with excitement and Wil enjoyed the control he had over his partner.

"Hup."

And with that small command, the Labrador Jake went to work. He'd throw up large chunks of mud and reeds with his feet and take a great leap splashing into the water, swimming hard. The dog never missed a bird and Wil gave him high praise with each retrieve. This was a duck hunter's dream, having a dog of this quality.

Wil and Jake took a great many birds and Flower was kept busy just preparing them for winter use.

As Wil paddled back to the cabin, he saw Flower outside cutting up firewood for the stove. He had a feeling that this was going to be a hard winter and they had better put up a lot of firewood. He thought that it would be nice to have a horse to help haul the wood to the cabin, but it still would get done anyway. There was a small cart he had found near the shed so he used that to bring in the wood. Several days of cutting, sawing and splitting finally got a respectable size pile of firewood.

The days of gathering rice were upon them and the labor of picking and poling took its toll on the two. The wild rice was all processed and by Wil's account, they had close to a hundred pounds set aside for the winter.

As the nights grew longer, it came time to put up some venison. If they could hang it in the shed, it would last for quite a long time. Flower figured that if they took three deer, it would get them through to spring. She wanted to smoke quite a bit so she built some small racks to hold strips of meat over a smokey fire.

One evening as the fall sun was setting, Wil walked outside to watch the last rays of sun sink behind the red and yellow maple trees. There was a warm breeze blowing across the water and he found a spot to lay down and watch. The colors were so beautiful that he could almost hear them.

Flower came to join him near the grassy river bank, and in the chill that followed the setting of the sun she snuggled closely to Wil, not wanting the moment to end. She had become his woman and the closeness she felt was unlike anything she had ever expected. She moved closer to him and with her hands on his face, kissed him softly. She had turned into a woman and had the feelings of a woman. In the darkness, she offered herself to the man she loved. They came together in the darkness and the world passed away below, both of them soaring through the night sky.

Morning coffee was a bit longer than usual, accompanied by much yawning. Flower joked about how Wil needed so much sleep in his old age. He grinned at her sheepishly. After what had happened last night, their lives would never be the same. He had had warm feelings for Flower before, but they had been more for a sister than anything else. Now that had changed significantly. For him this had to be a forever arrangement. He had thoughts of growing old with her and of having children. Wil was nearly twenty-six years old.

The day was spent getting ready for trapping and the coming winter. He paid close attention to things that indicated how bad the winter would be. Things such as the hairs on a woolie bear caterpillar and the size of the muskrat feeders indicated much to this veteran of the North. Their wood supply had been piled neatly and measured out at nearly seven cords. There was another cord of pine and pine knots for the cookstove. He had built a new door for the shed and decided to use it to store meat and smoked fish. It was a good tight building and he doubted that any critters could get inside.

Wil had spent quite a bit of time building them a new bed. It was stuffed with fresh straw and reeds and would eventually compress down some. As he put in the last of the reeds, Flower came in and covered the whole thing with a large blanket. Then she lay down and pronounced Wil's work to be a complete success. Their labor over the last eight weeks had been fruitful and Flower motioned for Wil to lay with her and rest. It seemed, though, that rest wasn't what she wanted and Wil found himself once again drawn to this most beautiful of Indian women.

Later in the afternoon when the pace of the day had slowed some, Wil decided to take a quick bath in the river. He found some newly made soap and a change of clothes and headed to the shore. He waded in to find that the water had turned very cold. He soaped up and washed his hair quickly. There was no time to waste just enjoying the bath. He rinsed one final time by dunking completely under water and walked out onto the bank to dry himself. He toweled off and put on his fresh clothes. When he came into the cabin, Flower joked about how blue his lips were.

The yellow dog Jake was always allowed inside at night and he had found a spot near the fireplace to warm his bones. Late one evening Wil heard Jake bark softly once and then nothing more. He wondered what it was that had stirred the dog so he walked out and lit a lamp. He peered outside through the window and saw nothing. Then he opened the door to look out and heard a muffled howl in the distance. The wolves hunted on this night and old Jake had better stay inside where it was warm and safe.

The cold weather of the season was now on them in earnest. Mornings found the river in front of their cabin frozen out several feet, but that melted in the morning sun. This season was what Wil waited for each year. Sometimes it was short in duration but in other years, it lasted several weeks. The daytime sun warmed the land enough to last through the night and any snow that did fall melted as it hit the ground.

October then faded to November and snow started to

accumulate in the shaded areas. Then one morning as daylight approached, it started to snow hard and kept it up for several days. Winter had indeed arrived on the Waboose River. Wil walked outside to see how bad the storm was and seemed quite surprised by how much snow had already fallen. The wind too had become part of this storm, blowing the new snow into high drifts in front of the cabin. Wil fashioned a pair of five-foot trail shoes to keep him on top of the snow while trapping. It took him quite a while to build them but the finished product was a work of art. Flower too wanted a pair for trapping.

In the days that followed the storm, Wil got his traps ready and he made some sets in the river for muskrats. As ice conditions allowed, he started to range further and further each day from their cabin. Some days, he'd leave before daylight and not get home until way after dark. When he came into the cabin, he'd be covered with snow and his beard frosted from the cold. Flower said that she was going to start trapping soon too. She would have her own trap line, setting snares for rabbits and fox. She was an experienced trapper and loved the outdoors as much as Wil did.

By mid-December the weather had turned brutally cold and if you weren't careful, any exposed skin would be frozen hard in seconds. Frostbite was a constant danger for them both. The year's trapping was going well and Wil had several nice pelts to sell in the spring. Evenings were spent stretching the big blanket beaver hides and getting them ready to sell. There was no teaching Flower how to do anything since she had done it all from a young age.

"What day of the week is this?" asked Wil.

"It's Saturday if I remember right," said Flower, smiling.

"I've been skinning beaver all week and handling those castors. I probably smell a bit ripe by now. What do you think about putting some water on to boil and getting down the washtub?" asked Wil.

Flower grinned at him. "I was hoping you'd say that," she said and laughed again.

Wil was a bit embarrassed. He was usually a neat and clean person, but the very nature of the work he did got him a bit grubby once in a while. Flower put on a large bucket of water on the stove to boil and another of cold water was brought into the house to warm. Wil put the washtub in the back room and got some clean clothes out.

"You're not going to wash up in there. You'll freeze to death," said Flower.

And with that, she moved the tub in by the fireplace. In an hour or so, the water was hot and Wil was ready to take a bath. There was one lantern in the cabin and it just barely lit the place. Wil carried the big bucket of boiling water to the tub and poured it in, making a large cloud of steam. Then he got the cold water to add to it. He poured half of it in and it seemed to be about the right temperature. Flower put another bucket on to boil.

Wil got the soap and a brush and started to get cleaned up. His hair was getting long and that took a while to wash. Without any notice, Flower came up to him and started scrubbing his back. He was still a bit embarrassed, but it was now time to put such things behind him.

Flower too got her bath and when Wil was a bit slow at offering to scrub her back, she chided him about not taking care of his woman. He grinned and said that he would always take care of her.

"We need a sweat lodge, Wil. In the spring I will build one," she said.

Wil had been invited into a sweat lodge before, but no women were ever allowed to go inside. It was a place where men met and a place where they had visions. It was a ritual for many of northern Minnesota Indians. This sweat lodge would be used to keep clean, and nothing more.

Winter wore on and the trapping had slowed down some.

An area this large contained only a certain number of animals and if you weren't careful, you could take too many and cut into the breeding stock. A trapper was a lot like a farmer in that he had to manage his herd.

December was nearly over and Christmas was just around the corner. One day he came into the cabin and said that it was time to go and find a Christmas tree. He was surprised when Flower said that she didn't know what Christmas was. Wil never missed the chance to talk about the shepherds and the three wise men. She hadn't heard about Jesus either so he told her all about his religion. She thought that it was the same as Gitche Manitou, but with different names.

Wil and Flower went out into the cold air and searched until they found just the right tree. He cut it down and they dragged it into the cabin. Wil fashioned a small stand for it and then told of how they made decorations for it. Flower thought it a bit strange to decorate a tree, especially one in their cabin. They made several stars and a lot of paper chains. Then came the part where Santa brought gifts for the children, but since there were none, maybe he would bring something for the two of them.

The next morning was Sunday, Christmas Day. Flower tried to sleep a bit later than usual, but Wil insisted that she get up and see what was under the tree. There was a very small gift sitting on the floor near the tree and Wil picked it up, showing it to her. She couldn't believe that anyone could come into their cabin without Jake making a lot of noise.

"Is it really for me?" she asked, holding it up for Wil to see.

"Now let me see. Yup, it's for you. It says 'Merry Christmas, Flower,'" said Wil.

Flower took her small gift and walked over to the kitchen table. She slowly opened it, not wanting the moment to end. When the paper had been removed, she saw that it was a small box. She opened it and inside was a thin gold chain with a beautiful red stone attached. Tears streamed down her cheeks and she smiled at Wil.

"Did Santa really bring that for me?"

"Sure looks like it to me," said Wil with a big smile.

He took it from her hand and placed it on her neck. It sparkled radiantly. And so this was Christmas.

In early April, Flower was running her line of snares. She had gotten three rabbits and the deep snow made her think that it was time to call it a day. As she came to her last snare, she saw a flicker of light brown and thought that she might have accidentally snared a deer. As she got closer, the animal in the trap gave out a loud low growl that scared her badly. She had snared a cougar and he looked like he was pretty mad, straining at the snare and trying to get at her. There was a small bit of blood coming from his foot and she saw that it was held by just his rear toes. He pulled extra hard and gave a sickening snarl as his foot came free. He was only thirty feet from her and closing fast. She brought up the 30-30 and shot just as he leaped at her. The bullet went right through his head and he lay motionless on the snow. She was only a few feet from the big cat. She had seen cougars before when she was a child, but not so far up north. She was only a mile or so from the cabin so she decided just to drag it back home without skinning it. It seemed to weigh almost a hundred pounds.

As she neared the cabin, she saw in the distance Wil coming in too, throwing up a mist of fine snow from his snowshoes. He could nearly run when wearing them. Jake was right behind him and when the big dog saw the cat, the hair on his back raised up and a low growl came from his throat.

"How did you..." Wil looked at what she was dragging and had a hard time speaking. "Did you trap that?"

"Well, kinda I guess. It got loose and tried to eat me so I shot him." She grinned broadly.

A pelt like that would bring a lot of money and Wil would see to it that she spent it all on herself. She was quite a woman.

Spring was getting some closer and now Little Bear was an

accepted member of the otter band of the Anishinaabe. He had trapped and killed many animals to feed his people this winter. He had been taken in by good people and they treated him as one of their own, even though he looked different than most Indians. He had light-colored eyes and a longer face. Many young women wanted him in their lodge but he did not want to offend any of the other men.

A friend came to talk to him one night and as they shared a fire and a pipe, he related how he had seen the tracks of a man in the snow, many miles from their camp. He told of where he had seen this and Little Bear kept it in his heart. It gave him a reason to think that his sister might still be alive. If there were white men in the area, they might have taken her to work for them. Most of the white men he had seen were bad and drank the whiskey that made them lose their minds. Some had many women to sell for a time. They were all dirty and had lice. If Flower was held captive by white men, he would have to kill them and set her free. He didn't like to cause such trouble, but there wasn't much he wouldn't do for his only blood relative, his sister.

Little Bear was far from being little. He stood an impressive height and weighed nearly two hundred pounds. His arms were large and the muscles in his back rippled like the water in the river. Several of his friends often challenged him to fight, but it was never much of a contest. They knew he would win, but wrestling was one of their favorite activities. Nobody was ever hurt and the object was to hold the opponent down for a short while so they couldn't move. The young women of the band all shouted his name as he wrestled and this made him feel good.

As spring approached, he readied his canoe for the season. It was in good condition and he put new pitch in the seams to keep out the river. The weather had changed and the river was rushing by, throwing water high into the air. Every once in a while, a large chunk of ice would try to get down the rapids and be torn apart by the rocks. This was a time of year when all men stayed off the river. It was much too dangerous for anyone. In the smaller streams, the men would wade in the cold water, chasing the big northerns. These were large fish and gave the tribe a much needed change in their diet. They would move slowly until they saw a big fish and then spear it with a lightning fast thrust. The children would try to catch the walleyes that ran in the fast water, but it was difficult with such hard current.

One way they caught them was to make a small channel in the streams that would guide the fish into a narrow area. This was done using rocks and logs. Once the fish were inside, they couldn't find their way out again and were easily speared.

In the springtime, the older men sat by the fire telling tales, passing along their knowledge. Several young men sat listening quietly as the elders spoke of the days of the buffalo and how they had all disappeared, leaving the plains bands wondering what had happened. The white men would shoot them with rifles and take the tongue and hides, leaving the rest to rot in the sun. Sometimes the white men would come across the prairie on trains. They sat on top of the railroad cars shooting and killing until their arms ached. These men had no reverence for life and eventually came in such numbers that the plains Indians were completely displaced. Many of the tribes had totally vanished. These were sad tales to tell but all the elders felt it was important that the younger band members knew their history and, even more so, could faithfully and accurately pass it on to succeeding generations

Women of the band also had their gatherings where their history was passed on from one generation to the next. Their history was rich with tales of women who stood proud, carrying the burning torch of past generations. Sitting closely together and talking softly, the words were spoken. Each woman was expected to pass the knowledge on and to teach the importance of their heritage. An important part of their gathering were the small children and babies. There were three infants barely a month old and they would hear these stories many times. These were all proud people, and rightly so.

The women of the camp were busy gathering sap from the big maple trees. As soon as the sun started to warm the maple trees, the sap would start to flow. Then the cold evenings, and freezing temperatures, would slow or stop it for a time. This was when the sap was at its sweetest. It was a long process that sometimes lasted for weeks. The sap was slowly boiled down and turned into a hard sugary rock that they all loved. Spring was a time to thank the Great Spirit for showing them the way through another hard Minnesota winter.

As the last of the snow melted, the men ventured further and further from camp in search of game. The word coming back was that they were finding a lot of deer that had starved during the winter. Near some of the forest openings, they would find three or four laying on their sides as if they had all died at the same time. North country winters always claimed a lot of animals.

The river started to slow some and Little Bear planned to take the canoe out the following day and look at the area where his friend had seen the tracks. It was a far journey so he took pemmican and jerky for the trip. He loaded his bow and several good arrows. As he pushed off from the bank, the river tried in vain to take him to the north. He turned the canoe in the current and looked to see his best course. The little birch canoe responded to his powerful strokes with the paddle and soon he was out of sight of the camp. The river fought him hard but his persistence ate up the distance. By the end of the third day, he had found a small stream that entered the Bigfork. He thought it might be the Waboose River. He camped once again for the night, making a small shelter of balsam boughs and dried reeds. He built a small fire to cook a duck he had shot and sat watching it cook. He felt good to be back on the rivers he loved.

As he sat in the quiet of the sunset, he tried to decide which direction he should go in the morning. Would it be further along the Bigfork or maybe he should spend time looking on the Waboose? Gitche Manitou was asked to guide his course. His thoughts wandered back to the people who had held him captive for so long. It seemed to him that they got much pleasure in seeing him cry as a child and he swore never to show that weakness again. He was now an accepted member of another band and as such owed them a debt that wouldn't soon be repaid. They had taken him in when he was cold and alone and given him food and a warm place to live. They were now more like his relatives. He dozed off with his head resting on his arm, the sounds of the river coursing through his soul.

He slept through the night and awoke to see a flock of geese winging across the Waboose, heading northward to their home. The colors of the sky and the smells of spring awakened his heart. He quietly slipped his canoe into the water and started to paddle down the small river. He had not been there before, but the trees and the river were all the same as they were near his home. He was far from his lodge now and wondered if he was searching in vain for his sister. She might have been dead for a long time already.

The first thing he noticed this day was a small stick poking up from an old muskrat feeder. It gave him a feeling of dread because this was a white man's way of trapping. It was probably from this last winter. He continued paddling for almost all of that day and saw no more signs. He seemed to have his senses tuned to the river, searching for anything that might look out of place.

He took time to do some hunting and saw a large flock of geese sitting in the middle of the river. His food supplies were dwindling to nothing. The flock was feeding and took no notice of his canoe drifting slowly upon them. He lay quietly in the bottom of the small craft and when he was so close that he could almost hear them breathing, he rose up and with an arrow already in place, took aim. As he moved, the whole flock saw him at the same time. He followed one goose and with a prayer for success in his mind, loosed the arrow. The sound of so many geese was nearly overpowering. The arrow found its mark and dinner fluttered back to the water, making a large splash only a couple yards away.

The rest of the flock was gaining altitude now and he paddled over to his prize. The taste of roasted goose was barely a memory from last fall. He found an opening on the river bank and built a small fire. The goose was cleaned thoroughly and while it roasted on his newly fashioned spit, he took the heart, liver and gizzard to cook separately. They were put on a smaller stick and held above the coals. Within just a short while, they started to smell an awful lot like dinner. He ate the heart first, relishing its delicate flavor. After he had eaten his fill, he sat what remained of his dinner close to the fire, trying to dry it for later use. Gitche Manitou had blessed him once more.

He paddled steadily up the small river, ever watchful for game. A small doe was wading in the river but as he got close enough to take a shot, the animal bounded for cover. From a canoe it would be difficult to get close enough to kill a deer.

Another muskrat feeder was found and it too had the same small branch stuck in the top. He was getting a bit concerned of what he'd find as he went around each bend in the river.

He made camp again that night before dark and ate some of his food, but not much. He didn't know when he might find more to eat. The dried goose meat still tasted good to him, but he didn't think it would be fit to eat in another day. He had no reason for a fire and sat quietly awaiting darkness and the next day.

As the night overtook his small part of the river, he heard something that caught his attention. At first it sounded like a child's voice. He thought for a time that it might be geese in the distance since the sound was the same, but it went away then as quickly as it had arrived, leaving him wondering.

The next morning he took great pains not to make any noise. He slid the canoe across the reeds and into the water as quietly as he could. This day, he paddled close to the shore and very slowly. After a couple hours of this he decided that what he had heard was indeed geese so he went back out into the main channel to make better time. As he came around a small bend in the river, he smelled smoke and quickly paddled back into the reeds for cover. He sat still, sniffing the air and listening. Then he heard the sound of a man's voice. He looked down at his bow and took out a single arrow, laying it across the string.

"Gitche Manitou, guide this man," he prayed.

He paddled to the shore and sat waiting once again for the night. As the darkness covered him, he slipped up close to the cabin and from a distance, tried to see inside. The smell of dog was there and it bothered him some. He climbed up on top of the wood pile, and stepped onto the top of the shed, giving himself a good view of what was inside the cabin. First he saw a large bowl sitting on a table. The glass of the window wasn't clear and it made him squint his eyes, trying hard to focus clearly. Then he saw a man walk near the lantern. He bent down and said a few words. Then a woman spoke softly to him, making him laugh. She had her back to Little Bear and he couldn't even see her profile. Then she walked to the other side of the table and turned quickly to face him. In the dim light of the oil lantern, he saw his sister Flower and there was no look of fear on her face. She appeared to be where she wanted to be and was happy.

Little Bear didn't quite know what to do so he just sat there in the dark watching the inside of the cabin. The man walked in front of the lantern and over to the door. A large yellow dog came outside and started to bark and run around, trying to see where the enemy he smelled was hiding. He was nearly frantic, barking loudly and eventually he came to the shed. He kept it up for a short while and the man came outside with his revolver drawn, trying to see what made the dog so excited. Jake kept barking and running in circles around the shed.

"You may as well come down now," said Wil, speaking Anishinaabe. "It's too darned cold to spend the night up there anyway."

Little Bear still lay quietly, trying to decide whether he should shoot an arrow into the man or talk to him. He decided to talk because his sister didn't seem to be in any kind of trouble.

"I am here," he said.

"Come on down and I'll hold the dog."

Little Bear came down from the roof and walked close to Wil. Jake was still making quite a racket. Seeing that the man meant him no harm, Wil asked him to come inside and talk. They walked up onto the steps and opened the door. Wil entered, followed by Little Bear.

Flower saw her brother and even though he had changed so much, she knew his face. She rushed toward him and Wil just got out of the way. They hugged each other for a long time and Flower cried large tears of happiness. At long last the two were reunited. They sat at the table and Flower introduced Little Bear to Wil. Little Bear was never prone to much laughter, but he was completely overtaken with finding his lost sister. He held her hand and they all talked for a long time. Jake still wasn't sure of this new man, but decided that it was all right since Wil wasn't in too much trouble.

"This is a good day," said Little Bear. "The Great Spirit has shown me the way to your lodge."

"You have changed so much, my little brother. You have outgrown your name." She laughed.

By midnight, they had all talked themselves out and decided to go to bed. Flower brought out blankets for Little Bear and he made up a spot near the fireplace.

"And where does my little sister sleep?"

"I sleep with the man who loves me," she said with a proud look on her face.

Wil looked at Little Bear for some sign of acceptance and found what he had wanted to see. It seemed that Flower's choice for a man was approved of by her brother.

The next morning Little Bear had gotten up quite early and left to retrieve his canoe. As he sat on the bank of the river watching the sunrise, Flower came out and sat down by him.

"What do you think of my man?" she asked her brother.

"He is a good man and his heart is good. Are you married to him?"

"No, but some day we will do that when we find a Holy Man to say the words. I stayed awake for a long time last night trying to think of a new name for you and now I have one. Just as you came out of the cabin, a great star cut across the face of the sky. From now on and for the rest of time, your name is Star Keeper."

"What is that in our people's tongue?" he asked.

"*Bustikogan.*"

Chapter 5: Rendezvous

Bustikogan stayed at the cabin for several days helping to get the furs ready to bring in for trading at the spring rendezvous. The trading post was a busy place this time of year and many trappers from far and wide came to sell and trade. The Hudson's Bay Company usually bought most of the beaver. Busti was quite good at handling the furs and Flower helped by putting them all in bundles. By the time that it was loaded with what they had, it nearly was too much for the big canoe. The trip to the fort was long and hard since the course was upstream and in the hard current of the springtime run-off. If the canoe tipped, it was a whole winter's work lost to the river.

"There's no way that we can get this all in one canoe," said Wil. "Are you interested in going to the trading post, Busti?"

"I am, but there may be some bad men there who we escaped from."

"We can handle that. No man can hold another against his will. That's the law in this country," said Wil.

Flower looked at Wil and said, "We may have a hard time convincing some people of that."

And so with the plan set, they divided the load between the two canoes and set off to the south and the trading post. Wil and Flower led the way and Busti with his lighter canoe followed. It wasn't that they expected trouble, but they were ready if something happened. Busti had his bow close by and Wil had the rifle sitting near his leg. Jake had his usual place, keeping watch for any wayward ducks that might come their way.

It was a four-day trip and the evenings were spent telling tales. Wil and his new friend Busti seemed to have a great friendship growing and this pleased Flower. As they sat near the fire on their first evening out, Wil started to tell of a time when he was young, a time when he and his friend Wilbur Withers hunted together.

Wilbur Withers was a most unusual person in that he seemed to have no fear. At the age of thirteen years, they had planned on a fall hunt for almost anything. Wilbur had brought a new tent with him this year and the two hunters set off by canoe up the Bigfork River. They had decided to make a kind of permanent camp and just head in a different direction each day. They found a small creek and paddled several miles, finally finding a good campsite. It only took them a short while before the new home was ready to move into.

The very first morning they decided to just paddle slowly, hoping to surprise something taking a drink of water. They had only gone a couple miles when they spotted a herd of nearly a dozen caribou crossing a stream. By the time they decided to shoot, the animals were already out of range. A plan was made and Wilbur was to try to head them off, turning them back toward the stream where Wil would be waiting in ambush.

Wilbur took his rifle and started to run through the boggy brush, throwing up a cloud of water drops as he went. Wil took the canoe to where he thought they might just cross and tucked it in close to the shore.

He had only been chasing the caribou for about a half hour and was started to get closer to them. They weren't going quite in the direction they should so he turned away from them, making a wider circle. He found himself going through some drier land and that gave him the ability to not only track better, but he made better time as well.

Wilbur looked up ahead and the entire herd was heading in exactly the right direction, right toward Wil. He decided to push a little harder and keep them going. It turned out to be the wrong thing to do. Near the back of the herd was an old bull that looked like he'd seen many a battle. Wilbur was closing now to only around fifty yards. The bull had a massive rack and was swinging it side to side as if he was tiring of this game.

Wil stood up a little above the grass to see better. The sight that greeted his young eyes was nearly unbelievable. The big bull turned in his tracks and charged Wilbur, bringing the entire herd with him. Wilbur saw him coming and raised his rifle to kill the huge caribou. Just as he pulled the trigger, the animal hit him full force, throwing him into the air. It didn't look like the caribou was about to fall over so Wil, from the river, took a shot at him. Nothing happened. The caribou seemed like he had Wilbur on the ground and was trying to gore him.

Wil got out of the canoe and headed toward the caribou herd. They were slowly milling around, not quite knowing in which direction to flee. The bull still was working on Wilbur when Wil steadied himself on a small piece of driftwood and with one shot killed the massive beast. The rest of the herd finally got their bearings and trotted off into the nearby woods. As he got closer to the dead animal, he heard something and stopped to listen more closely.

"Can you get this damned thing off me?" asked Wilbur. There beneath the huge head was Wilbur, laying really close to a log. He had been hiding there since the animal started in on him. He didn't seem a lot worse for wear, but he did have a large black and blue area on his back side where the animal had lifted him from earth to sky, depositing him in the boggy swamp. He figured that a caribou of that size was worth a little suffering.

"You know, when I lifted that big caribou head to let him out, Wilbur wasn't even breathing hard. He wasn't a bit shaken. It seemed that nothing ever bothered him," said Wil.

Busti and Flower had been listening closely and when Wil told the part about being pinned down by the caribou, they both laughed hard. It seemed that neither had ever heard of such a thing, but a good story was always appreciated.

On the evening of their third day as they sat watching storm clouds gather far to the west, Jake started barking and there didn't seem to be a reason for it. A short while later they saw a large canoe with four men heading toward them, paddling hard upstream. The men all wore beards and appeared to be trappers. As they saw Wil standing on the bank, the man in back spoke and the canoe came toward him.

"Ah. *Bon soir, mon ami.*"

Wil waved and the men paddled close to the bank.

"You go to the rendezvous?"

"Yes," said Wil. There was no room for light conversation. The man understood that these were tense times until the furs were sold.

"Maybe we see you there and we can drink some whiskey."

"Maybe," said Wil.

The men in the canoe were most interested in Busti and Flower and watched them closely as they pushed off back out into the river's current. Wil and Busti took turns throughout the night watching for trouble.

The next morning before the sun started to come up, they were back in the canoes for the last hard push to the post. The weather looked like it was going to drop some rain on them. As they got near the fort, Jake would bark once in a while when he heard something. Then they came around the last bend in the river. It looked a lot different than it had the last time they were there. Many canoes lined the bank and men slept nearly everywhere. There appeared to be a hundred campfires and the Hudson Bay Company met them before they even got out of the canoe. The man wore a beaver top hat and spectacles and carried a large pad of paper. He was very skinny and it looked like his pants were about a foot too short for him. As Wil used to say, he was the kind of man who would have to stand twice in the same place just to cast a shadow.

"Do you have beaver to trade?" the man asked.

"We do, but not now. We'll look around first," said Wil.

Busti didn't exactly fit in with the rest of the people there. He wore buckskins and had his long hair neatly tied in back. On his waist he wore a knife and a small buckskin bag. Busti stood head and shoulder taller than most of the trappers. He rarely smiled and as such gave the appearance of being quite a fierce man, and not one that they would want to argue with.

Flower stood beside Wil, but didn't give the appearance of being his woman. She too stood tall and straight and looked each person she saw directly in the eye, fearing none. She also wore a knife on her waist. Her eyes went from one person to the next, looking for any of the men who had held her captive for so long.

There were many teepees with traders all shouting for attention. Many dollars had been paid out for fur and these men all wanted their share. Closer to the shore and furthest from the trader's row were the sellers of whiskey and women. There was no law here and people were sold like any other commodity, just not quite so openly.

The two men, one woman and a yellow dog walked around for a time, always with an eye on their canoes and furs. Flower saw several things that they would need to purchase and Wil nodded in agreement.

Wil looked over at Busti and said, "Can you watch our furs for a bit? We need to go talk to the clerk in the office."

Busti nodded and walked toward the canoe. As he got closer, he saw a man cut the rawhide strap on top of a pile of their furs. He lifted a few and tried to pull them free. The man turned to see if anyone was watching and then turned back to the furs. Busti ran at him and when he got close enough, grabbed the man's hair, bending his neck back and holding his knife snugly to the man's throat. Slowly the man sunk to the ground, afraid to speak or move. Busti kept the pressure on the knife. Just a slight sideward movement now was all that would be needed to slit his throat.

By this time, Busti had drawn quite a crowd and the uproar brought Wil and Flower back to the center of the activity. Jake saw what was happening and bit the man on the foot for good measure.

A small man in a black hat came running toward them yelling for that "damned Indian" to let his brother go. He lifted a pistol from his belt and started to aim at Busti. Then all hell broke out again with Wil holding another of his group with a knife to his throat.

"You think we should kill 'im, Wil?" asked Busti.

"Not yet. What happened, Busti?"

"This *cheechuk* tried to take some of our fur."

"Naw, I wasn't gonna take yur fur. I was just lookin."

The man was having difficulty talking with his head pulled back.

Wil let the second one go and as he stood, he kicked him in the rear just to get him moving. Then he threw the man's gun into the river. Busti still had a firm grip on the first man's hair. He looked at him very closely.

"Next time I see you, I kill you quite dead. *Nes pa?*" said Busti.

The man scrambled to his feet and followed his brother to the far edge of the camp.

"He was pretty close to meeting his maker. Maybe now he'll get religion," said Wil. "If nothing else, that'll keep the rest of them at a distance."

Wil and Flower once again tried to go into the post to check on his prices. It was as he had suspected. All of the prices had been raised to take advantage of the trappers' good fortune.

"Take that squaw outside."

Wil turned quickly to face the clerk, the same one he had had the problem with before.

"I thought we settled that," said Wil.

The clerk recognized Wil and turned back to his work.

"How come you raised all them prices?"

"That's called business, mister. If you don't like it, the next post is eight days' paddling from here."

Wil was getting a bit peeved, but he was a good trader himself.

"What you giving for blanket beaver?"

"Depends on the quality. I'll take a look at what you got if you want me to."

With that the man took his pencil and paper and followed them out the door, locking it behind him as he left.

"Which is yourn?" he asked.

"All of it," said Wil with a slight grin.

The man laughed. "No. I mean which pile is yourn?"

"All of it." This time Wil wasn't grinning.

The clerk started at the top of the first bundle. He measured it and smelled it and Wil wasn't sure that he might not want to eat some of it as well. He went through a bunch of facial contortions and offered Wil ninety cents. Wil looked at the man in disgust and took the pelt from his hand.

"No sale," said Wil with a look of utter disdain on his face.

The clerk took another one and went through the same process, measuring and smelling.

"Eighty-five cents."

"No sale."

There was an awful lot of fur yet to go through and Wil figured that unless something changed drastically, they would end up over at the Hudson's Bay trader. The clerk came up with a dollar for the next one and Wil took if from him, laying it back on top of the pile.

"Sure am glad you came to look at our fur, but you may as well head back to your work. You and I won't be trading this year," said Wil.

Busti walked close to Flower and whispered in her ear, "Watch this."

The clerk shrugged his shoulders and started to walk back to his price raising. "It's your loss, pilgrim. I made you some good offers."

"You did indeed, and I certainly do appreciate it, but they're just not good enough. If we take that price, we'll starve next winter. We spent last season under some balsam boughs to keep warm and was hoping to get enough to buy a sack of beans."

"Ya, sure ya did," he said and he laughed. "Well, maybe I can do some better. Lemme take another look."

And with that the trading got going in earnest. The price for their blanket beaver soared to over a dollar and a half and the muskrats all fetched thirteen cents. There were some martin, fox and three wolf hides as well. The amount was starting to get into serious money. Then when they got to the end of the pile, the clerk wet his pencil and added up the whole thing. It came to just over $240.00, but they weren't done yet.

"Now there's the part of them high prices in there. If you drop the price of what we buy by half, we might just have a deal," said Wil.

The clerk looked at him quite seriously. "You strike a hard bargain, Wil Morgan."

The clerk extended his hand and the two had a deal. Wil would get all he needed and the clerk would make a profit as well. Both parties seemed happy with the outcome.

Night was closing in and they got a small fire going to cook some supper. A man came by selling smoked turkey legs and they bought three for their dinner. As they sat enjoying their meal, Flower remembered the cougar pelt and asked Wil what he was going to do with it.

"Well, as soon as them men over there start to drinking a bit, I'll show ya," said Wil.

Night wore on, and on the far edge of the gathering, somebody broke out a fiddle and started to play a tune. Several ladies were let loose upon the throng and many spent some of their hard-earned money for twenty minutes in a small tent. At five dollars each, they made a lot of money.

Wil took out the sack with the cougar hide and climbed up on a table. He drew his .45 and fired a single shot into the air. The whole place became quiet.

"Last winter my woman trapped a cougar. You'll find one hole in the hide, right betwixt the eyes. She shot it with a 30-30 to keep from getting et. Now I wanna know how much you men of the river'll pay for sich a hide."

A murmur started in the crowd as the men talked between themselves. Then one said that he'd give four dollars for it. Another said that he was a crazy man. Then it went to ten dollars, an unheard amount for any fur. Wil got down and let the men feel of the rich fur. The bidding then went to fourteen dollars. From a ways off, Wil heard a man say thirty dollars, followed right away for a bid of fifty dollars. Now they all wanted to be the owner of such a pelt. Nobody had even seen such a thing before. Finally it rested with a bid of an even hundred dollars from the Hudson Bay trader himself. This was the most that anyone had ever paid for any pelt anywhere. Wil took the money and handed it to Flower.

"Now you have a problem. You have to spend all of this on yourself," said Wil.

"I cannot do this," she said as she tried to hand it back to Wil. "It is too much money."

Flower had a most serious look on her face. It was indeed a lot of money, but to spend it all on herself would be difficult even for her.

Later as they all wandered through trader's row, the trapper they'd seen on the river approached Wil.

"And how is the price for beaver this year?"

"It's not as good as I wanted, but it could have been worse."

"We have many furs to trade. It was a good year for us," said the trapper.

"Sorry I didn't invite you in back on the river, but ya just don't know who you'll meet near a rendezvous," said Wil.

"We had a gun on you too," said the man and they both laughed.

The man held out his hand and introduced himself. "I'm Robert Roulet."

"I'm Wil Morgan."

They shook hands and talked for a while, mostly about trapping. It seemed to Wil that this was just another hard working trapper and a good man.

"Stop in to our camp later and we can drink some whiskey."

"Thanks. I'll do that. No whiskey, though. It makes my head spin." They laughed.

The next day as the sun rose, the sky filled with ominous looking clouds and a lot of thunder in the distance. It looked as if they'd be getting wet on their trip home. Wil had planned to do all of his buying on this day so Flower would do the same. It lasted nearly all day with a lot of haggling over prices. The trader got nearly all of his money back and had a young man bring all their purchases to the canoes. By the time it was loaded it was nearly dark, so they decided to spend one more night at the post. Wil had purchased a small canvas and as it rained, the only ones that enjoyed it were the ones with either a tent or a canvas. It rained by the bucket full and it looked like it was going to keep it up for quite a while. Behind them, the river had once again come alive with all of the new water.

By ten o'clock that night, the rain had eased up and then stopped, letting Wil walk around some. There were still a lot of people selling things that they'd made.

"You want a girl?"

Wil turned to see who it was who was talking to him. It was a neatly dressed man in a top hat. His voice made Wil feel some kind of recognition but his face wasn't familiar. He felt a slight uneasiness building deep inside his chest, but he refused to let it out.

The man leaned toward him once more. "She's only about ten and she'll earn you a lot of money," said the man.

Wil couldn't believe what he was hearing. It was against every law there was to sell another human, especially a child. Wil thought to ask how much he wanted, but thought better of it. He still was having a hard time with this. He had visions of a little Indian girl being held captive. Then he thought back to the last time he saw his mother alive. Was this the man who had gotten away? Was this the man who had killed his mother?

"Lemme see her," said Wil.

The man lead him to the very back of the makeshift village and into a large tent. There huddled under a coat in the corner was a young oriental girl, wide-eyed with fright. In the dim light of a coal oil lantern she appeared to be around nine years old.

"Two hundred dollars. You take her and do what you want. Two hundred dollars. Alright?" said the man.

Wil was feeling his short temper start to grow, and he tried hard to keep it in check. This was a time for cold hard thinking. He had the money to free the girl, but then what would she do? She was far too young to take care of herself. He wished Flower was there to help. The man looked at him impatiently, waiting for Wil to make a decision.

"You want her or not? I got other men who would pay double that amount."

"I dunno. That's a lot of money," said Wil, buying time.

Thoughts raced through his mind like a fast river. He had to do things right. If this was the man who had killed his mother, he'd have to be sure. He didn't want to be tried and hung for murder.

"I'll take her. What's her name?"

"Who knows! She can't speak no English anyway."

Wil handed the money to the man and held out his hand to the little girl. She started to sob and whimper. She thought Wil was another customer who would hurt her. The man reached to take his jacket off the girl and Wil grabbed his wrist. Jake started to move closer to the slaver.

"Leave it be, mister." His voice was more of a growl than anything else. "Get outta here and take yur china doll with ya."

As they walked back outside again, it started to rain some more. The little girl shivered from the cold. She kept trying to get away from Wil and when she saw Flower, she ran to her for protection.

"Where did you find this little one?" she asked Wil.

Jake walked over to her and licked her hand. Busti saw that she was a little different than he was used to and asked what tribe she was from. There was again no answer.

"We gotta get the canoes loaded and head out right away," said Wil. "The man I got her from will be trying to get her back pretty soon so they can sell her all over again. We'll have to paddle hard and get out of this area."

In a short time, they had left behind the noise and smell of the trading post. Wil was nearly broke, but Flower still had some money left. The little oriental girl huddled in the bottom of the canoe trying to keep warm in the steady downpour, waiting for the man who had sold her.

Chapter 6: Sum Chi

The stormy sky opened some to reveal the night stars and with it came a warm breeze out of the south. Wil, Flower and Busti paddled hard all night and by first light were several miles from the trading post. There was no doubt in Wil's mind that they were being followed by the girl's former captors. White slavery was nothing new in the remote parts of the north.

Wil signaled to Busti to pull into shore. As they got out of the canoes, Wil told Flower to see if she could dig out a couple cans of beans. They were all pretty hungry and cold beans out of a can would do well to refuel their bodies. The little girl went with Flower into the woods for a time and when she came back her hair had been combed and she looked a bit more at ease. Busti handed her a can of beans and a spoon. She ate slowly, and it was easy to tell she hadn't had food in quite some time.

Flower and the girl finished their meal and sunk the cans in the river. Jake got a hunk of biscuit and that would have to do him for a while. Busti called Jake into his canoe to help even out the load a bit and they were ready to start again, but as they pulled out from the bank they paused for a moment to see if they had left any indication that they'd been there. The men who were following them would be looking for any sign that they'd come that way.

As they paddled, Flower kept talking softly to the little girl, but she gave no indication that she understood what was being said. Flower pointed to herself and said her name several times. Then Wil did the same thing but it brought no response from the little girl. The sun was getting high in the sky and the temperature had been steadily climbing for the entire morning.

No words had been said for over an hour. From nowhere, a small voice broke the near stillness.

"Sum Chi," said the small girl, pointing at herself. "Sum Chi."

Wil grinned and said her name, making the girl smile shyly. He felt that there was hope now to find where she had come from. It was a puzzle to him how a girl so young could be so far from her home.

They kept up the same mile-eating pace for several more hours and just before it got dark, Wil motioned to Busti to pull up onto the river bank.

"We need to make camp for the night, but no fire yet. We'll pull the canoes up into the brush quite a ways," whispered Wil. "No talking either. Ya can hear a man's voice for miles at night."

Wil turned to the girl and put his finger to his lip, telling her to be still.

"*Mai put*," she said, whispering.

Wil got a puzzled look on his face.

They rested in the dark until the morning sun started to

lighten the sky and then headed out once more, trying hard to evade the men Wil knew were chasing them. This little girl quite probably had been sold many times and was their meal ticket. They wouldn't give up without a fight. In just a short while, they were back at work paddling downstream and making good time. Still Wil thought about the little girl and wondered what could have brought her all the way to northern Minnesota.

As Wil paddled along in silence, he tried hard to recall anything and everything about his mother. He recalled the shape of her face, the softness of her touch and even her voice calling him for supper. It seemed to be so long ago. He thought of a time when he had wandered too close to the river and had fallen in. His mother had seen it happen from across the yard and came running, diving headfirst into the water to rescue him. Then he thought of how she spanked him for being so careless. It seemed to be so very long ago. If the man he had bought Sum Chi from was the man who had killed his mother, he'd kill him and that was a certainty. No matter how long it took him, he'd kill him.

Their trip was wearing hard on them all and by the time they were getting close to home, they were all in need of rest. The days had been tough, even for Wil. They were in their third day on the Waboose and by noon saw the last bend in the river before the cabin. Wil looked over at Busti and grinned at him. The race was on, Wil and Busti racing to see who would get to the cabin first. Wil's canvas and cedar canoe was much heavier, but he had a second paddler in the canoe and she held her own in any situation. The little girl grinned as they raced, saying something like "*Lao lao*."

Wil was falling behind and in just a few minutes Busti ran up onto the bank, the proud winner of the race. They were all quite tired and Flower got out of the canoe and just fell down on the bank, glad to be home. Sum Chi lay beside her, watching the men unload the canoes. They had evaded the men who chased them and it felt good to be back in their own part of the world. When they had left the trading post in the middle of the night, Wil didn't think that anyone had seen which direction they had gone. He was starting to feel safe again.

All of their supplies had been moved into the cabin and now needed to be sorted and put away for later use. They had bought an entire one-hundred-pound sack of flour and that was put into a heavy wooden barrel. Clothes had to be stacked and traps put away for winter use. Everything had its place. Sum Chi was starting to feel like this might be her home for at least a short while. Jake took to following her everywhere she went and she seemed to really like the big dog. Busti too was starting to like the little girl.

The spring weather turned to the warm days of summer and their little cabin looked more and more like a home. Flower had put up new curtains and the place took on a new look. Sum Chi was starting to talk a bit more and seemed like she really wanted to learn their language, but every once in a while she would get excited and let out with a whole string of gibberish no one could understand. They just stood and watched her until it passed, and then they would all laugh.

Within a few weeks, Flower was able to teach Sum Chi enough to carry on a conversation of sorts. One evening they went out to sit and watch the sun set and Sum Chi started to talk. Flower found out that the little girl was actually eighteen years old and her mother and father had died on a ship when some men boarded it and took her prisoner. Her family was very well to do and were from Siam. She had spent many weeks in San Francisco working for a man who bought her. She was put up for sale each night to the sailors and was expected to make money for her owner or she would be beaten badly. She remembered being sold several times to different men and her life was always hard. The last man who owned her had kept her for nearly a year, selling her and then getting her back again several times. Flower listened and understood what she was saying. They both had been victims of bad people and forced to work or be beaten. When Sum Chi understood that Flower too had been stolen as a child they both started to cry, holding on to each other. "Life can still be good for you, Sum Chi. We will take care of you until you decide what you want to do."

Busti and Sum Chi spent a lot of the summer together fishing, hunting and gathering berries. The girl seemed to love the outdoors and wouldn't come inside until it was dark. There was getting to be a closeness between them and Busti did his very best to impress her. Flower had seen Busti change and at the age of twenty he seemed ready to take a woman for his own. He cared for Sum Chi and she watched out for him in every way.

The little oriental girl was now dressing like the rest of them and her hair was combed back and braided. She too wore a knife on her waist and moccasins on her feet. She had made quite a transformation form a scared little oriental girl to a confident, but still small, oriental girl. She spoke nearly as well as the rest by summer and worked daylight to dark.

"Tomorrow I go back to my people. Will you go with me, Sum Chi?" asked Busti.

She nodded and with that she had in essence decided to spend the rest of her life with Busti. He was a strong man and a good provider. Life for her would be much different from what she was used to, but she knew that no matter what happened, she would be treated right. Her days of being bought and sold were over and nearly any kind of life would be an improvement. She knew that she couldn't stay with Wil and Flower forever and she had fallen in love with Busti. It was the right thing to do.

The next day, they loaded their possessions into their canoe and started off toward Busti's village a few days away. Wil and Flower were sad to see them go and it seemed strange that their new family had just been cut in half. Life did take some strange twists and turns. Not many weeks ago, Flower thought that she was all that remained of her band. It was strange indeed.

━━━ ━━ ━━━

Busti and Sum Chi made the trip to his home in just three days. She was getting pretty good with the canoe and he was proud of her. As they pulled up onto the shore, many children and women came running to see them. They all touched Sum Chi's face and smiled at her. It was clear that this was Little Bear's woman.

That evening they sat outside by the fire telling stories of how he had found his sister Flower and her man. The Holy Man said that he would go see them sometime during the summer so that he could say the words for them. Busti was glad to be home. The trail he took this year was much different than he thought it would be. He had found a good woman and a new friend, Wil Morgan. The entire village listened until deep into the night of the things Busti had seen and done.

"Some very bad men were chasing us from the trading post. Wil thinks that one of them killed his mother long ago. He will be hunting for him and we may need to help him. They are the ones he rescued my woman Sum Chi from."

"Are you going to make this your woman?" asked the Holy Man.

"Yes. We have talked of it and we will stay here with my people," said Busti.

"Tomorrow we will say the words."

Everyone went to their lodge that night and an old woman took Sum Chi's hand, leading her to a lodge in the middle of the clearing. Several women followed them inside.

The next morning Busti looked around for Sum Chi and didn't see her anywhere.

"Old woman. Where is my bride?" asked Busti.

"You have no bride, Little Bear," she said and grinned at him.

He laughed too and then realized that no one knew his new name. He looked for the Holy Man and told him that his sister had given him a new name, Bustikogan. The Holy Man did not know the name because it was from another tribe.

"I am Star Keeper, Bustikogan."

"Bustikogan," said the man, rolling the name around on his tongue.

That afternoon as the sun was high, the Holy Man called the entire camp together. Bustikogan stood in front of the Holy Man and nervously looked around for Sum Chi. Then a woman gave the signal and she came outside. She walked up next to the Holy Man and stood as tall as her small size would allow.

"Do you want this man for your husband?"

Sum Chi looked up at him and said, "Yes. I want him."

He turned to Busti and said, "Do you want this woman for a wife?"

"I want her," said Busti.

The Holy Man took each of their hands and joined them together.

"Then go in peace and have many babies," said the man.

Another woman opened the door of the largest lodge and motioned for them to go inside. They entered the lodge and with that, they were married. No other man would ever touch Busti's woman. That evening they made a large fire and everyone wore their finest clothes. Some of the young men wore porcupine headbands and fine feathers. Others wore beautifully stitched buckskins. Some of the women wore jingle dresses that tinkled when they moved. This was a big occasion and since it was summer and a time of plenty, they feasted for two days. Busti had come to their camp as an orphan and now both he and his wife were accepted members of the clan.

The summer days for Busti and his new wife took on a whole new routine. They were hunter gatherers and were forced by the land to prepare for the winter even though it was several months away.

One late afternoon, Busti was paddling quickly down the river. He had been hunting and was coming home empty handed. Game had been scarce for several days. He rounded a turn in the river and before he could turn his canoe, he had nearly run into a large cow moose with her head down, feeding on the river grass. The confrontation was sudden and the moose had a calf near her, making it a very dangerous situation. Busti got the canoe turned some, but before he could get away, the moose hit the small birch canoe with her front feet, cutting several holes into the canoe. Still Busti tried to paddle away but the cow was intent on destroying the small craft and him as well. She kept hitting the canoe and in just a short while she had it in pieces, with Busti trying hard to swim to the other side of the river. She saw him and gave chase. Busti swam with all the power he could muster, but the moose was overtaking him quite rapidly. He looked over his shoulder and saw that he was just inches from her hooves so, taking a deep breath, he dove under the surface of the river, swimming hard, trying to get away from her. He kept swimming until he had to come up for breath and surfaced almost next to her. They saw each other and she turned once more with blood in her eye, ready to kill him. Busti took another deep breath and swam away again. In a short while his lungs ached from lack of air and he surfaced once more. This time the moose and he had chosen different directions. He took another deep breath and swam further away. When he surfaced, the moose was nowhere in sight; she had rounded another turn in the river.

He got to shore and stood surveying his situation. There was a small cut on his forearm and another on his left leg. Altogether he considered himself to be quite lucky. These were huge animals with bad tempers.

His canoe came floating by him, one small piece at a time. The moose had shredded it. He was still several miles from his home with no supplies and darkness was nearing so he decided to head for his camp.

Darkness overtook him, but he kept walking. By morning's first light, he walked into his camp, greeted only by the now awakened dogs. Sum Chi tended his wounds and made him some food for his breakfast. He had survived a close call but he had lost his canoe and his favorite hunting bow in the process.

Gitche Manitou had been good to them and Bustikogan was starting to feel drawn to the things that the Holy Man of their clan taught them. There was much to learn but Busti thought he might want to do this. He was quite young for such a thing, but if the people agreed, he would start with his apprenticeship soon.

Sum Chi, as the wife of a clan member, was not allowed to speak of holy things. She spent most of her time in tribal projects, tanning hides and gathering foods to be dried. Busti started to go with the Holy Man wherever he went. Sometimes it was to watch over the passing of an old friend. Sometimes it was to gather plants for healing. This was a hard thing for any man to learn and sometimes it took several years. On one occasion, Busti was lead to a place far to the north where white mud boiled and bubbled to the surface of the ground. On another he followed the Holy Man to a gathering of tribes where the red rock used to make pipes was harvested. His brothers the Shoshone, Sioux and Mandan all came from far away to gather the rock and at a certain time of the summer when the moon was full, they all met in this southern part of Minnesota. This was a holy place and even if there were problems between some tribes, no war making was allowed.

One evening as the sun set, Busti was asked if he wanted to go into the sweat lodge with several men. He thought that it might be a chance for him to learn more so he accepted and was lead inside. The lodge was made of many small branches that were tied together to form long poles, and these were pushed into the ground in a great circle. The sweat lodge was shaped like an inverted bowl nearly twenty feet across. On top of this framework were laid many blankets. Then inside they placed several hot rocks that had been in the fire for many hours on the ground. Once the men were all inside, the last of the blankets were put on the frame and the temperature inside started to climb. A pipe was passed from one man to another in the circle. Busti puffed on the pipe a couple times and passed it to the man next to him. It was the great chief Little Crow from southern Minnesota. Busti had seen him earlier in the day and had been told of his bravery in many battles.

As the temperature continued to climb for a couple hours, some of the younger men fell over from the heat. Another man would check on the fallen man and if they thought he was in trouble, they would sprinkle some water on his head.

Late into the night as the rocks cooled, the men would come outside and sit by themselves to discuss what visions they had seen. Busti listened in silence as the elders spoke of great things ahead for the Red Man. Their lands would flourish and their lives would be better. Busti had thought for a time that he too had seen a vision but he didn't want to speak of it in front of these great men.

Busti and the Holy Man paddled up the Minnesota River to the Mississippi River and all the way to the great lake Winibigoshish. From there it was a short portage across the continental divide to the Bigfork River.

One evening as they sat by the fire, they discussed their trip.

"Why has Bustikogan been so quiet this day?" asked the Holy Man.

"I have many thoughts running through my mind. When we were in the sweat lodge, I had a vision and I didn't want to tell the rest of the men there."

"What was your vision, young Bustikogan?"

He sat for a while, still not quite sure he wanted to share what he had seen with this elder, this Holy Man. He had never seen a vision before and he thought that maybe he had just been dreaming.

"Most young men keep their visions to themselves for fear of looking like a child having bad dreams," said the man.

Busti felt deep inside that the vision was for him to share. He took a deep breath and started to speak. "In the harvest moon, some men will come who are very bad. A woman will be taken. I did not see the faces or I would go and kill them now. These will be bad times for us all."

The Holy Man sat staring into the flames.

"It is not young men who usually see visions, but this sounds like the Great Spirit is speaking just to you. Be careful, Bustikogan, and keep these things deep in your heart."

The trip down the Bigfork was somewhat of a relief for the two since they had spent many days paddling upstream. Now to just paddle slowly with the current was appreciated by them both. As they got close to the Waboose River, they thought to spend a couple more days and stop in to see Wil and Flower. Soon they approached the small cabin and saw smoke arising from the chimney. Jake was barking at them and Wil came outside to see what all the commotion was. Then Flower saw her brother Busti and ran to him, giving him a big hug.

"It seems that you have been eating well, my sister," said Busti.

"Yes. We have much food." Then she realized what Busti was saying. "We have a child growing in my belly," she laughed.

She was a thin woman and her belly was indeed starting to show the new child.

They all laughed for a time and Wil too joined in. It was good to have company and they all moved into the cabin.

"I will cook for you," said Flower. "You must stay for a time so we can talk."

Busti nodded and looked at the Holy Man. He too was a large man and his many years showed in the lines and creases of his face. An old battle wound had left a deep scar across his forehead and his hair was as white as the summer clouds.

"It has been a long trip for us and this old man needs to rest for a time."

That evening, they sat outside on the river bank talking about all that they had seen and the great men they had met. The Holy Man asked if they still wanted to be married. Wil looked at Flower and grinned. They did and they decided that tomorrow was the right day to do it.

At sunrise the next day, they stood on the bank of the Waboose River holding hands. The Holy Man said the words and with that they became man and wife. There was a permanence to their lives now. They wanted to stay right where they were and raise a family and if the Great Spirit would allow, they might even see grandchildren. Wil kissed his wife and she held him close. Not long ago, she had no idea that her life would take such a turn. Even Wil, who was so used to being alone and making his living from the river, had no thought that his life would turn in this direction.

Their time together was spent mostly just relaxing and talking. In the evening they would have a campfire and speak of days long ago. The Holy Man told of a time when the tribes of the plains came, trying to take their lands. Many battles raged for several days with a lot of wounded and killed. His father was among the dead.

One night the entire village was sitting around a campfire talking and laughing. Times had been good for the tribe and they saw no need to post sentries. Even the tribe's dogs had grown lazy. As the smoke arose into the night sky, a war cry tore through the darkness and an enemy still unseen loosed a large number of arrows into the gathering. Then another great war cry brought the enemy to the firelight. The Sioux raiding party had already killed nearly a dozen people, and among them were several women and babies. What was left of the band of warriors drew their knives and tried in vain to defend their village. It was a one-sided battle with many deaths. Several young women and children were taken.

By the time the sun rose in the morning it was clear that their band had been nearly all killed. The Sioux were the victors this time, but there would be many years of back and forth battles and many good men would die. It was a dark time for the Anishinaabe, but sunrise for them was getting closer. Within three years the Sioux had all been driven out of Minnesota and once again a time of peace and quiet would prevail. The lesson had been learned well, though. There would never again be a time when they would let their guard down.

Busti listened carefully and took it all to heart. It would be his responsibility now to pass this on to the next generation so that they could remain strong. The story had once again been told and with that, the Holy Man had fulfilled his obligation to past generations. He arose and went inside to sleep near the fireplace.

Busti and the Holy Man left the Waboose River and paddled the three-day trip back to their village. It felt good to be getting near their camp again. As they pulled up on shore, several children greeted them and offered to carry their supplies to the camp. Soon the sound of drums greeted them, welcoming them back home. The chief spoke with them for a time and then it was Sum Chi's turn to see her husband. Busti had been gone for nearly a month and she quietly led him into their lodge.

Inside where no one could see, she kissed him softly and told of how she had missed him. She brought a cloth and warm water from near the fire. With her help, he removed his clothes and lay back on the blankets. She bathed him completely, drying him with her hair, and then bathed herself. This was a very special woman and her customs suited him well.

Chapter 7: Two Bad Men

The man who had sold Sum Chi to Wil wasn't about to lose his livelihood without a fight. His plan was to sell Sum Chi to Wil and then reclaim her by any means, only to be sold again. He had done this many times and had plans for it continuing for quite a while. His partner was a sailor from San Francisco called Dirk. He was a modern-day pirate and had stolen many girls for the slave trade. They would hike a distress flag up the mainsail and a passing ship would come to their aid. As soon as the boat got alongside, the pirate crew would storm aboard and kill the captain and anyone else that would fight or even complain. It was easy pickings for slavers, because most people thought the days of pirates had passed.

On this particular day, the sea was calm and the steamship *William Harden* was making good time toward California with a crew of nine plus the captain. They were heavily loaded with passengers and cargo. They had taken several passengers from Siam and were heading on to the island of Mindinao for a load of fine silk. The company would pay a good bonus to the captain and crew for such a good profit and short sailing time.

In passenger cabin number six there was a family from Siam. The father was a medical doctor heading for San Francisco and a big convention. After that he was going to enroll in a college to further his medical training. The mother was a beautiful woman in her forties. There was also in that cabin two children, a boy of nearly seven and a girl of sixteen. Each evening of the trip, Mr Pao Sung would open a small trunk and bring out a small statue of Buddha. Their religion required them to pray to Buddha at least once a day and to burn incense during their prayers. The captain of the ship had received several complaints about the smoke, but never felt that it was enough of a problem to stop it.

On toward dark, the first mate sounded the alarm to the captain that he had spotted a distress flag on a small ship they were passing on the port side. As they got closer, they saw a single man dressed in white waving to them. Their boat was making smoke as if it had a full head of steam, but there was no forward motion at all. There was something wrong with this and the captain was a bit on guard. His first thought was that they had lost their prop or broken a prop shaft. He ordered the *Harden* to swing wide and come alongside slowly, into the wind. The first mate kept a watch through his binoculars and noticed that there were no other hands on deck.

As the *Harden* contacted the pirate ship, the man in white blew a whistle and a gang of ten men stormed out of the hold. Their first duty was to secure the *Harden* alongside their boat. The rest of the crew went over the side to find the captain and crew. The pirates were all armed with pistols.

The captain of the steamship *Harden* reacted much too slowly to the alarm. He headed to the wheelhouse, locking the door behind him. One of the pirate crew broke into his cabin and shot him through the head. Then it was a search for the first mate. They found him trying to open the arms locker and killed him as well. The man in white gave an order that the whole crew should be lined up on the starboard side for his inspection. Two men guarded them and then the rest of them went searching for the passengers.

In a span of time no more than five minutes in length, the whole ship had been secured. It was nothing new for this pirate. He was unshaven and wore a dirty white coat and trousers. He had apparently stolen some captain's hat and must have thought it made him look pretty important. They'd been at this for several months now but just recently had moved closer to the United States mainland. Their usual hunting grounds were near China and Japan.

The man paraded up and down the deck of the *Harden*, hands folded behind his back with a smug look on his face. The passengers were quite afraid and their only protectors were nowhere to be seen. He walked over to see the crew and asked if any wanted to join his ship. Hearing nothing, he ordered them all shot. The ensuing sound of gunshots scared the passengers badly. The pirate walked back to see the passengers. In his estimation, there were four that would bring good money. All of the rest would cause him trouble. He walked down the line and with his cane pointed to the ones that would be taken. First there was a woman of probably twenty-five years. Then there were two young ladies of around fourteen years. Then there was Sum Chi.

"Take them to my cabin and tie them up," the man in white told one of the men. "Keep watch on them until I get there."

Overhead, the sky was a bright burning blue dotted with small puffy clouds. Several large white birds swung back and forth lazily over the top of the two ships. The peaceful scene belied the tragedy unfolding below on the *Harden*. Each time there was a gunshot, the birds would fly a distance away only to return in a short while.

The captives were all bound fast with light rope and helped over the side of the *Harden* to the pirate ship. Then the pirate turned to his crew.

"Kill all the men."

Shots rang out once more and several bodies crumpled onto the deck.

"You have done well, my men. Now let's look and see what else they may have of value."

They searched the ship and found several weapons and many cases of wine and liquor. They took several crates of food and silk. The captain seemed satisfied with their find and gathered his men on deck.

"The ship and the women are yours. Tomorrow we burn it to the waterline but for now, she is yours."

The men all cheered and immediately headed for the remaining ladies and girls. There was much screaming throughout the night and by morning the entire ship was silent. They had killed several women and the remainder would die in the fire. They took a gallon of coal oil and sprinkled it liberally over the floor of the engine room, leaving a trail to the deck.

"Set the fire," called the pirate captain. "Cast off the lines."

And with that, they started to pull away from the *William Harden*, and the ship immediately became engulfed in flames. They saw that two women had jumped into the ocean and he ordered that they be shot in the water. The fire grew quickly, extinguishing the pitiful screams of the passengers. Then it heeled over and went to the bottom, leaving little more than a wisp of smoke on the horizon.

They were still a couple days from the coast of the United States and plotted a course and speed that would bring them in near midnight.

The four captives spent the ensuing nights at the mercy of the pirate captain. He used them at his will and passed them around to the crew. Young Sum Chi had seen the rest of her family killed and now was alone in the world. Such degradation was quite unbelievable to someone of her social standing and she kept thinking that maybe someone might rescue her. Everything around her was filthy and smelled terrible. It seemed to her that no one bathed and in a very short time she felt lice crawling on her.

Some time during the night, she was awakened by a kick in the ribs. A man motioned for them all to come with him. They were led up a gangplank to the dock and then hustled into the back of a horse-drawn covered carriage. Their trip was frightful and all four of them cried softly, not knowing what awaited them.

After a trip of more than an hour, the carriage made a sharp turn and stopped. Sum Chi heard some voices and a man opened the back of the carriage and motioned for them all to come out. They stood in the darkness and a woman dressed in a heavy black coat held a lantern up to each of their faces.

"What's your price for the lot?" asked the woman.

"Well, this is a good bunch, Mabel. The price is high cuz they're all so young."

"Don't give me that crap. What's the price?"

The pirate captain walked in front of them again, looking them over.

"A thousand each, Mabel. That's the best I can do."

She laughed. "Sounds to me like you're trying to retire after this bunch."

"Well, I'll go to eight hundred a piece, but that's about as low as I can go."

"I dunno. That little one would probably die soon anyway," she said, pointing to Sum Chi.

"Tell you what. You buy them three at my price and I'll throw in the runt for free."

With that, Sum Chi entered into a life of prostitution and all that went with it. For nearly a year she was used and abused by many men. The only good that came from it was that she was always kept clean and fed well. Then she started to get sick often and one day was sold to a man who was a regular customer.

Her life once again had changed. They went by train northward and then eventually to the east. She was never allowed to speak to the other passengers and didn't know their language anyway. If she looked around, she was pinched hard.

The journey lasted for several days and then they came to a big city called Minneapolis. She saw several people who looked like her, but before she could talk she was hustled away to another dark room to await her master's wishes. One day she heard him approach and he opened her door. Standing there was a different man in a top hat. Cash was exchanged and Sum Chi was once again sold into a different life.

Two men took her to a big river and she started northward in a canoe. At each stop they made, she was sold and then later the man would come and steal her back again. These were bad men and didn't hesitate to kill. Eventually she was taken to a big fur rendevous in northern Minnesota. The men were nearly all dirty and just wanted to use her for a short time. Money was always exchanged for her services.

Her current owner was a man called Bart and the other was named Dirk. One evening, she was offered to Wil Morgan for two hundred dollars and with that she regained her freedom. The man who had brought her there must be looking for them, since that was the way he operated. As she sat in the canoe, she expected to hear a shot ring out at any moment. It took her a long time to get over that.

The night after her release from captivity, Bart and Dirk asked around if anyone had seen them leave in the night.

Nobody had seen a thing so he flipped a coin and chose the wrong direction to start looking. His course took him many miles away and through many small rivers. By mid-summer, he was nearly ready to give up. They decided to head the other direction and spent many days paddling in search of their property. There were some opportunities for robbery and murder, but still they found no sign that their girl was near.

One evening as they paddled a small river, they heard the sound of laughter off in the distance. Sum Chi and Flower were sitting on the bank of the river laughing.

Their men were on a hunt for caribou and had been gone for several days. Sum Chi had planned on staying with Flower only for a few days and felt that she should have left the day before. She wanted to be home when Busti arrived. Her clan had a lot of work to do and she was needed there.

The men watched the cabin closely for nearly two more days and were sure that Sum Chi was one of the women they had seen. No other men were around and Jake had been taken with them on the hunt.

The pair waited down river and when it got almost dark, they walked through the woods up to the cabin. There was no light inside and they figured that everyone was asleep. Quietly they sneaked up on the small cabin and when they were on the step, they yelled and kicked open the door. Inside Sum Chi peeked out from the small room and then jumped back in. Flower had grabbed her pistol and came out to face the intruders. She had the hammer cocked and was raising the gun when Dirk fired at her with his shotgun. Flower fell backwards into the bedroom, landing on her bed. Sum Chi immediately knew by the look in her eyes that Flower had been killed. She made it past the men and ran out into the night, leaving Flower all alone, bleeding badly. The men chased her in the dark yelling for her to stop, but she was scared and kept running as fast as she could, hour after hour, mile after mile. She had recognized the men and swore that she would rather die than go back to the life she had before. She just kept running in the darkness, the thorns and vines tearing at her clothes.

Back at the cabin, it was once more quiet and serene. Flower was having trouble breathing and blood was running from her mouth. The shotgun had hit her full in the stomach, killing her baby. Soon it would take her life too. Her eyes fluttered, and with each breath she made a gurgling sound. Within just a few moments, she lay still. Her life blood had ran out onto the floor of their cabin and with that, she and her child began their journey. Gitche Manitou awaited them on the other side. Flower held her boy child in her lap and paddled her white canoe northward through the stars, to the home of the Great Spirit.

Chapter 8: The Hunt

Sum Chi had made the trip between their camp and Flower's home several times. She was heading to her village, walking rapidly along the river bank. Each small noise she heard made her dive for cover. For nearly three days, she continued her journey and arrived home in the middle of the night, nearly starved from lack of food. She had gathered some berries and nuts, but that was nearly all she had eaten. As she told the story to her people, they became angry and wanted to go looking for the men who had killed Flower.

Morning found the men gathered on the river bank waiting for the blessing of the Holy Man. He said the words that made them safe and each canoe started their search for the men who had killed Flower and her child. Busti and Wil were still away and didn't know of her death yet. For several days, the clan looked for the men who had killed Flower and her child. Then, as their supplies ran low, they came back to the camp. Sum Chi was still quite upset and spent a lot of time alone in their lodge waiting for the return of Bustikogan.

Wil had left Busti where the Bigfork River met the Waboose. He paddled hard for two long days, their canoe heavy with meat and hides for the winter. He knew that Flower would be waiting for him on the river bank, waving and smiling.

He approached the cabin just as the sun was setting on the river. Jake barked in excitement. There was no one standing on the bank so he yelled Flower's name. Still there was no response. He thought it strange and kept paddling. As the canoe hit the bank, he ran up to the cabin steps. Then he saw the open door with a broken latch. Wil walked to the fireplace and lit the lantern. As the flame grew he saw blood splattered on the wall. Jake was whining and refused to come into the cabin. Then Wil threw back the curtain on their bedroom doorway and saw the unspeakable. His woman, Flower, lay dead on their bed. Her eyes were wide open and sunk deeply into her head. The smell was nearly overpowering. A large pool of dried blood covered much of the floor.

Deep emotion started to take control of his soul. His wife, his future, was laying in the cabin, dead from what looked like a shotgun blast. Who could have ever wanted her dead! She caused no one any grief and always treated the people she met with kindness. He thought back to when she had saved his life by killing that old trapper. It just didn't make sense. Everyone there was glad to see the old man dead.

He sat in the dark on the river bank trying hard to understand who could have killed her. If it were the tribe she had been a slave to, they would have taken her, but never killed her. Sum Chi had been with her too and he wondered if the men who at one time held her could have done this. That had to be the answer. It was the men he had bought Sum Chi from and the one who had killed his mother.

Now Wil Morgan stood at the first crossroads of his young life. All of the plans he had made with his wife were destroyed. He would never feel the small hands of his child touch his face. His wife would no longer laugh and make his life so full. No longer would she come to him in the dark of night, making his life complete.

He sat very still in the darkness for several hours thinking, then his grief would overtake him and he would begin sobbing once again. His last companion Jake sat with him, his head laying quietly on Wil's leg. There was nothing here for him now. The cabin that they had found love in now had no use. He once again walked inside.

Wil covered Flower with a clean white sheet and started to look around for anything that he might need on his journey, his search for her killer. He found Flower's pistol on the floor, cocked and ready to fire. Wil picked it up and examined it. No shot had been fired. He would need his traps, his guns, and his clothes plus several items for his day-to-day existence. He put them all into the canoe and walked back inside. He searched each and every nook and hiding place for things he might need in the future. Over the door was the shotgun right where he had found it. He might have need of it. He had no idea where his trail would lead him and he wanted to be prepared. He might need money, so he went to where they had buried old Charlie's cash and dug it up. In the light of the coal-oil lantern he opened the box and retrieved the roll of money. It didn't feel so important right now.

Wil walked one last time back into the cabin and then into their bedroom. He touched Flower's now cold hand and once again, tears flooded his face. His head hung low, he walked slowly to the fireplace. He took the coal oil lantern in his hand and walked to the door. Wil looked around for Jake to make sure he wasn't in the cabin. Then with the strength of extreme anger, he threw the lantern to the floor. Coal oil ran in small rivulets across the planks and he watched for a moment as the entire cabin caught fire. The blaze grew rapidly and Wil retreated toward the canoe. He stood on the river bank, now alone once again. He motioned for Jake to get in and pushed the canoe out into the water, paddling a short distance out into the bay. He turned for one last look as the roof of their home collapsed, sending tongues of flame and sparks high into the air. Great waves of sadness washed over him and he turned his back and paddled away. The sky was just beginning to lighten and the reflection of the fire showed itself as it flickered off Jake's yellow fur.

In the light of morning, the tear-streaked face of Wil Morgan had dried. Now it was pure hatred that welled up from deep inside him. He would find who had killed Flower, no matter how long it took. His first job, though, was to find out what had happened to Sum Chi. He wondered if she had been taken again or if she had gotten away.

Wil paddled night and day until he reached the camp of his friend Bustikogan. He arrived in early morning, nearly spent from his time paddling. He hadn't stopped for food or rest since he had left his cabin. The people from the village came down to the river bank to see him and when he looked up, he saw Busti walking toward him. He walked straight to Wil and put both arms around him. Wil nearly bust into tears again, but then busied himself, pulling the canoe up on shore a short way. Then he saw Sum Chi walking toward them.

They sat down on a log and talked for a while and Wil discovered who it was that had killed Flower. It was indeed the men who had held Sum Chi for so long. She had only seen their faces for a short time, but she knew right away who they were and what the gunshot had done. The man Dirk had killed her. She told of how the men of the clan had searched but found nothing.

Wil thought for a time of all that had happened. This man who had killed Flower was most likely the same man who had killed his mother. Now he would have his revenge from this bastard, this killer of women.

It was time now to make a plan. He couldn't just run off in several directions searching. He had to be methodical in his hunt for these men. It was nearing noon and Wil said that he had to rest for a while. Busti brought him to their lodge and made a place for him. They gave him fry bread and meat and then he covered himself with a blanket and slept.

Near nightfall, Wil awoke once again and went outside to see the men of the clan all sitting by the fire. There was much discussion of where to look.

The next morning, the men of the clan all set out once more in search of those killers. They looked for anything that would indicate a direction of their travel. For several days they covered different streams and rivers, ranging far and wide. They all agreed to come back in four days even if they had found something. At the end of that time they all returned with no idea of where the killers were. There was again much discussion.

"I'm going to search for these men myself. I'll be leaving in the morning," said Wil.

"I will go with you," said Busti.

"This is my trail. It is my wife who was killed and you have a wife to take care of," said Wil.

"We are almost brothers. Your grief is my grief. Your loss is my loss. My sister was lost and I found her. Now she is with the Great Spirit. We will search together in the morning. Your trail is my trail."

Busti spoke in a most forceful manner and Wil came to understand the depth of his loss. His sister was the very last of his family.

By next morning's light there was a severe thunderstorm and even in the face of such wind and lightning, the hunt began in earnest. Jake sat in the middle of the canoe. Busti was in front and Wil took the back. Their weapons were simple. Busti took his bow and the knife he always carried. Wil had his .45 Colt and the 30-30 Winchester. There were plenty of rations, enough to last several weeks if necessary. There was dried fish for Jake, usually sled-dog food, and that would keep him going for a long time.

They slid the canoe into the water and turned it to face upstream, their direction of travel. Wil sat in back steadying the small craft for Busti. The big man got in and took up his paddle. Turning to face Wil for a moment, they locked eyes. Each man spoke of the seriousness of the trail they were about to take. One or maybe even both of them might not return here, but that was all right too. This trail was of such importance.

On the shore, nearly a dozen men stood watching until the canoe disappeared down the river. The hunt had begun.

Having a good supply of food meant that they didn't need to hunt as they went. They covered a lot if distance, both men quite determined.

The first night, they paddled slowly in a light rain. They wouldn't have been able to sleep anyway. Dinner was served a bite at a time, both men chewing slowly on hard pieces of jerky. By daylight, the rain quit and they went ashore and built a fire to dry out. Each man found a place to sleep for a time.

By noon they were both awake and the sun was making the place feel like a sweat lodge. A quick meal was eaten and the trip resumed with both men well rested. Even Jake seemed to feel a bit more like traveling.

Their journey gave Wil and Busti a long time to think. For Wil it was a serious battle with his hatred trying to devour his logic. He sincerely wanted to be the one who killed Dirk. If those men were still in the area, someone would have seen a sign of them. You couldn't cover that much territory without turning up something.

After several days, they came to the trading post. It had changed dramatically. The weather was turning colder and fall was in the air. Frost hung around in the shade for a couple hours after the sun rose. There were no canoes pulled up on the bank. Smoke rose slowly from the storeroom stove pipe. That was the only thing that gave any indication of life here. Wil and Busti walked inside.

"No Indians allowed in here, dammit."

Wil was in no mood to listen to this and ran right at the man, drawing his knife as he went. The little clerk turned to run but Wil caught him by the shirt, throwing him to the ground. A knife was pressing not too gently on the man's throat.

"Now you son of Satan, we're gonna talk. If you give me what I want, you might live to see tomorrow, but I won't guarantee it."

The little man nodded.

"Did you see two slavers come through here lately?"

The man nodded, fear written all over his face.

"Was one wearin' a top hat?"

He nodded again, moving his head only slightly.

"Did one have a shotgun?"

Once more he nodded, hoping he'd given the right answer.

Wil let the man up and dusted off his vest.

Jake stood near the man, a low growl coming from deep inside.

"Which way did they go from here?" asked Busti.

The man was slow to answer and Busti hit him hard across the face with an open hand. He fell to the ground once more, anger seething from his lips. It was apparent that he held a lot of hatred for Indians. Jake was growling too but this time he was only an inch from the man's throat, waiting for his master's command.

"It don't appear that you're going to live through this, mister, unless you start to cooperate real quick."

Wil looked down at his dog.

"Easy, Jake."

The dog backed off a short distance, still keeping an eye on Wil, still waiting for a command.

"Those men killed my wife and I want 'em," said Wil, boiling with rage.

"I'll tell you everything I know," said the clerk, getting back up off the floor. "Just keep that dog away from me.

"They came here a couple months ago and got damned liquored up. Said that they were looking for a China girl that got lost. Then they came back somewhere around three weeks ago. They got liquored up again and said that they were going back to California. That's about all I know," said the clerk.

"Which way did they take?" asked Busti.

Once again it seemed that the clerk wasn't going to talk to Busti, but when he moved toward the clerk, the little man started to talk again.

"I remember that they said something about Minneapolis."

That set their course. If it was Minneapolis, there were darned few ways that they could go. They would probably try to catch a ride on a paddle boat south on the Mississippi. From there it was anyone's guess. Trains were a good bet if they had money, otherwise it was rivers. Wil bet on the rivers and Busti agreed since they probably didn't have much money. Slavers made good money unless they lost their girls.

Wil didn't know the face of one of the men, but the man with the top hat stood out in his mind like it was just yesterday. By now he was certain that this was the man who had murdered his mother and he would have to be killed. He was certain too that he would enjoy it.

They didn't need many supplies since they were pretty well provisioned already. Wil bought some rope tobacco and a bottle of cheap whiskey. Busti jerked the lid from a small barrel of pickles and ate them as Wil walked up and down the big room. The clerk was still keeping an eye on Busti, mentally adding up each one as the big Indian ate. Wil picked up one more box of .45 caliber ammunition and some candy. Then he went up front to pay.

"That'll be two dollars ten cents and a dime for his pickles."

"I'm not paying for his damned pickles. You get it from him," said Wil.

The clerk started to say something to Busti and then thought that maybe it just wasn't worth getting knifed for a couple damned pickles.

They left the trading post and loaded the rest of their purchases into the canoe. The course had been set and the plan made. Busti too swore vengeance for his only sister. They would paddle hard as long as their bodies could take it and then rest. They'd run these two into the ground and kill them. Now it was down to vengeance. It was going to be a hard trail but each man was driven in his own way to see this to the end, no matter how long it took them, no matter what the outcome.

━━ ━━ ━━

As the two slavers left Minneapolis, they seemed to be paddling just fast enough to steer their large canoe. They had spent several days and nights in a brothel by the river, drinking large quantities of whiskey and consorting with the women of the night. Their supply of money was starting to run short and they were on the hunt for another victim to rob. They had thought to kidnap one of their prostitutes but didn't want to deal with their keepers. The pair was filthy inside and out and the only thing that could clean them up was whiskey and a good thunderstorm.

"Dirk. Pass me that damned bottle."

"What bottle? I drank the last of it two hours ago."

"You bastard!" said Bart. "I should have left you back in the city."

They kept up their measured pace even though winter was right behind them. If they got caught in a big freeze, they'd have to spend the winter wherever they were. That might mean starvation. Between the two, they had only forty-two dollars, but that was enough to get them a ticket on a train to San Francisco. Warm weather and the possibility of a new girl appealed to them. They decided that they would catch the train whenever it crossed their path. Red Wing, Minnesota, was their next stop but it was another two days until the westbound train came in.

The first thing was to sell their canoe and that brought them another ten dollars. Things were starting to look some better now and they heard that a brothel was only a block away near the only saloon in town. Saturday night found the pair full of cheap whiskey, and talking way more than they should. They purchased the services of a prostitute and took her to their hotel room. There they drank and talked, again way too much.

By the time the train was due, they had sobered up some and purchased their tickets to San Francisco for eight dollars each. They were leaving a trail a blind man could follow, all because of their fondness for whiskey and women.

Once on the train, they started to look for a new victim, card game or just plain robbery and murder. It didn't matter to them. They found a small man who was quite well dressed and figured that he would have carried some money. Dirk tried to strike up a conversation, but the man kept to himself. The plan was set. They would wait for him between the cars and when he came out to use the restroom, they'd kill him and take his poke.

Near ten o'clock at night most of the passengers were asleep and Dirk was in position. As the man walked down the isle of the train, he seemed to be quite sleepy. He needed to use the privy and as he opened the door between the cars, he saw Dirk standing there like he was waiting his turn. The man closed the door behind him and just stood there waiting his turn in the near darkness. Then the door to the privy opened and Bart came out. The little man was between the two slavers and in just a moment Dirk covered his mouth and a knife pierced his chest. Bart held him up and his partner quickly went through the man's pockets. Finding what they wanted, they turned and dumped his body out onto the siding. It rolled and toppled end for end, stopping near the edge of a small lake. The train just kept rolling, dark smoke trailing behind.

The men took turns coming back inside and sat quietly. Their efforts had netted them nearly twenty dollars, an amazingly small amount of money, they thought. His wallet showed that he was a corporation president and should have been carrying much more. They were a bit puzzled.

Morning found the pair well on their way to warmer weather. The conductor noticed the empty seat and by noon realized that the man was no longer on the train. The next stop in Des Moines, Iowa, had the local police boarding the train looking for the dead man. Everyone was questioned and then the train pulled out, heading for Omaha. They would never find out what had happened to the man.

Nightfall had the train stopped in Omaha, Nebraska, for a five-hour layover. The two white slavers went to a restaurant and had a quick meal. They walked across the street to a nearby saloon for some whiskey and more conversation. They seemed to get drunk quite easily and in their love for talking, nearly missed the train. When they got back on, they immediately fell asleep and didn't bother anyone for several hours.

The train whistle blew loudly and Dirk awoke with a start, drawing his pistol from his belt. A lady across the aisle saw the gun and when everything had settled down some she went to see the conductor.

"Those men got a gun," she said, pointing to the again sleeping pair.

"You mean those two way in back?"

"Yes. I saw it myself."

"You go and sit down and I'll see what the engineer wants to do about it."

She walked back and sat down, still watching the pair. After an hour, the conductor motioned for her to come up front.

"We're nearly in Denver now and when we get in, we'll talk to the authorities."

She nodded and went back to her seat.

Denver, Colorado, was a big city and the train station was huge. There was another layover of three hours and this was just enough for the two to loosen up their mouths some more with cheap whiskey. The sheriff found them in a nearby tavern and asked if he could talk to them.

"Where you boys heading?" he asked.

"Well, we're going to San Francisco looking for work," said Bart.

"What kind of work do you do?" asked the sheriff.

"We do most anything," said Dirk. "Why do you ask?"

From the other side of the room, four men playing poker stopped and just watched to see how this would play out.

The sheriff was used to handling the rough men that came through his area and grabbed Dirk's arm, spinning him up against the wall. He had his forearm across Dirk's throat and with the other hand reached inside his coat, pulling out the small revolver.

"What do you do with this?" he asked.

Dirk didn't know quite what to say.

"Empty your pockets out on the bar."

Dirk did what he was told and pulled everything out except for the knife. The sheriff seemed quite interested in the date that he had bought the train ticket.

"You see a little guy wearing glasses on your train near Des Moines?"

"No. Not that I remember," said Dirk, and Bart shook his head in agreement.

"Well, I got a little story for ya," said the sheriff. "Somebody knifed a corporation president on the train the other night and stole his billfold. They figure he had around twenty dollars in his pocket. Whoever did this took the man's money and dumped him off the train. Funny how damned dumb that killer was. He missed the five thousand dollars the man had in his money belt. A fisherman found him the next day laying on the bank of a lake nearly dead. He knows who knifed him, too."

The two slavers made eye contact, but only for a second.

"I'm going to take you two in for questioning," said the sheriff.

There wasn't much time left for them to act. The lawman was reaching for his handcuffs and in just a few moments they'd be in custody. Bart took a quick swing at the lawman, hitting him on the temple. He went down to the floor with Bart right on top of him. Dirk grabbed his gun off the bar and shot the lawman in the face, killing him. The other men in the bar had long since evacuated the place and they turned to go out the front door. Just as Dirk grabbed the door handle to go outside, he heard a scream and turned to see a barmaid standing over the dead sheriff, squalling loudly. He thought to waste a moment and go back to kill her but there was no time. They straightened out their clothes and tried to walk calmly outside. They blended into the crowd and disappeared.

Chapter 9: River Search

Wil and Busti were making good time and within a week were nearly to Minneapolis. They pulled into the river bank one night planning to get some much-needed rest.

"This looks like a good place, Wil," said Busti.

"It does, and I could sure use a cup of coffee. I wonder how far ahead those two are?"

"Could be a long way, but we made good time. Maybe tomorrow we get to the big city."

They started to unload the canoe in the near darkness and Busti got a fire going. They opened some canned stew and pulled out some soda biscuits to go with it. After a quick meal, Wil unrolled his blankets and snuggled up under the overturned canoe. Jake found a comfortable spot near the men. There was always time for conversation.

"I think when we get there, I'll ask around to see if anyone remembers them coming through," said Wil.

"Maybe they're still there."

"No. I think they headed back to California. We've got a long journey ahead of us yet," said Wil.

There wasn't much doubt in Wil's mind about who had killed his mother, and he knew the man's partner was the one who had killed his wife. His mother was a good woman who would never hurt a soul. She was liked by everyone, but that didn't matter to the slavers. All they wanted was money and they used people to get it. She apparently had fought bravely and that had gotten her killed. She was too proud to live the way the slavers wanted. She must have figured that it was a choice between getting away from them or getting killed and she accepted that. Her choice was that she would not be made a slave.

When Wil was sixteen, his father left again to be a ship's captain. Life on the river without his wife had been a terrible hardship for him. Wil got letters from him once in a while with money enclosed. By the time Jonas Morgan left to sail the oceans once again, Wil was well educated and was most certainly able to take care of himself.

The money that Captain Morgan sent now went into a bank in Minneapolis in the name of Wil Morgan. Wil could withdraw funds at any time he wished, but the independence most men seek was not only a goal for Wil, it was a reality.

Now it had been over a year since he had heard from his father. He could have been on a long voyage or maybe even killed. He would inquire at the bank as to when the last deposit was made into his account.

They slept well and in the morning awoke to see frost covering nearly everything. Their little spot under the canoe was the only place that wasn't frosted. In the near darkness, they ate a quick meal with coffee and then reloaded the canvas and cedar canoe again.

Noon found the two in the middle of the big city with buildings on either side of the Mississippi as far as they could see. Then Wil noticed a place called the Pig's Eye Saloon. That would have to be the first place they headed for. They pulled the canoe up on the bank and walked into the bar, Jake right beside Wil.

An old man was behind the bar, busy washing glasses. There were few customers around so early in the morning.

"What can I get ya?" he asked Wil.

"Ya got lemonade?"

"By gum, I think I do. How 'bout your friend?"

Busti nodded and Wil grinned at him. He had never been in such a place and the whole smell was quite overpowering to him.

The bartender brought them two tall glasses and sat them on the bar.

"What is this?" asked Busti.

He had never tasted anything like this before.

"It's a drink made from lemons. They grow way to the south of here," said Wil.

"Anything else, boys?" the bartender asked.

"Well, I am looking for some information. We're chasing a couple white slavers who killed my wife a few weeks back. I don't know much about them except for the name Dirk. One of 'em wears a top hat and they both drink a lot."

"That could cover a lot of men, but in this case, I do remember them. They stayed for a couple days drinking and chasing the ladies. One morning they came looking for something to eat and said that they were going to San Francisco. Then they just disappeared, and we never saw them again. I do remember that they came here in a canoe and that's the way they left."

Wil and Busti drank down their lemonade and thanked the bartender for his help. As they got back outside Busti took off his shirt and shook it out, trying to remove the smell of the place. He eventually replaced it with a fresh one from his pack. Wil laughed at him.

"Those places all smell like that," said Wil.

"It smells like something died in there, a long time ago." Busti wrinkled his nose in disgust.

One thing that still bothered Wil was the question of whether or not his father was still alive. If he was still sending money into the bank account, at least he was still alive. The name of the bank was Cattleman and Merchant's but he had no idea where it was. A man was sitting on a park bench reading the paper.

"You got time for a question or two?" asked Wil.

"Sure. I'm just waiting for the street car."

"I need to find the Cattleman and Merchant's Bank."

"Well, I'm heading there myself. It's only about a mile from here."

"Mind if I tag along?"

"Course not. You got business there?

"I just need to look up an old account," said Wil.

In just a few minutes, the street car came by and stopped. Wil paid a nickel for the ride and sat down to watch the scenery go by.

The man he had spoken to got up and stood by the door, ready to get off when the car stopped. Wil figured he better do the same. As he stepped back up on the sidewalk, he looked around for the bank. He was standing almost in the doorway. There was a revolving door and he wasn't quite sure how to use it until he watched a few people go in. He followed their lead and found himself in the lobby. A guard watched over the crowd, ready in case someone wanted to withdraw money they didn't own. There sure were a lot of people. He stepped forward and waited in line.

When it was his turn, he stepped up to the next teller.

"I need to find out if any money has been put into my account," asked Wil.

"I'll need your account number," said the woman.

"Well, I don't recall ever having one."

"I'm sorry, sir, but you can't take money out or even make an inquiry without the account number."

Wil felt a small degree of anger starting to grow. "Now listen. I need information and I need it now."

His voice was starting to sound a bit impatient. One of the guards heard Wil start to raise his voice and moved over closer to him, ready if there was any trouble.

"Maybe our bank president can help you."

She walked over to a closed door and knocked. Then she walked in. A few seconds later she came back and took a piece of paper from a box.

"I'll need your name and address."

Wil wrote down what he was asked and stood waiting. In just a few minutes, a man came up to him. The man from the trolley car stuck out his hand.

"Good to see you again. I understand you have some money here. Come on in and we can get to the bottom of this."

Wil and the bank president talked for quite a while. It seemed that twenty-five dollars had just come into his account in the last week. Deposits were infrequent, but they indicated that his father was still alive.

"Where did the money come from?" asked Wil.

"It was transferred from a bank in Australia."

"How much money is there in my account?" asked Wil.

"Well, let's take a look. The account has been open now for a number of years and including the interest we have paid, you have a total of $4,043.13, and that includes this month's deposit."

"That's an awful lot of money."

"Yes. It is. Did you want to take some out of your account?" asked the man.

"No, but I sure would like the address of the bank the money came from."

"I guess I can handle that."

Wil and the bank president concluded their business and Wil went to wait for the next trolley heading back to where Busti waited. He was a rich man thanks to his father. When this search was over, he'd take some of the money and go try to find him. After so many years of wondering if he was alive, it gave him a good feeling to know that he might still have a family. He thought to tell Busti of all he'd learned, but thought better of it for now.

They got back to their canoe and pushed off, paddling hard to get out of the city. Neither of them felt comfortable with so many people around them. Both men had spent nearly their whole lives seeing few other people.

The canoe came around a sharp bend in the river and they saw another small town off in the distance. It was getting close to dark once again so they thought to make camp outside the town. All through the night, they kept hearing the sounds of the railroad and the factories. The foul odor of coal smoke wafted over them all night long making Busti wish for the clean air of the Bigfork River, so very far away.

As morning came to the river, the first thing they noticed as the sun rose was that there were no birds chirping around them. It was way too quiet. The sun warmed them quickly and it looked like they would have a warm day to paddle. There was something different about this place. Wil went to the river to get enough water for a pot of coffee and when he was walking back to the fire he smelled something. He put his nose to the water and it had a bad smell. Even Jake wouldn't drink water from that river. This was a bad place and they got the canoe ready and paddled down stream to the town.

Again there was a saloon so they decided to ask for information once more. Busti said that he'd stay and watch the canoe and their supplies. Wil grinned. Busti didn't want any more of that stink he'd found at the last one.

In a few minutes, Wil came back outside and sat by Busti

and Jake on the river bank. The smell of the air was different.

"They had been here, alright, but it was several days ago. The barmaid said that the whole town of Red Wing breathed a sigh of relief when they got on the train."

Busti looked up at Wil and grinned.

"They stayed at the hotel for a couple nights. I'm going to go and see if I can get a couple names and anything else they'll tell me. I'll be back in a few minutes. Jake—stay."

Wil walked up the hill to street level and over to the Cattleman's Hotel. The place was just as dirty and smelly as the rest of what he'd seen on the river. The hotel clerk looked up when Wil walked in. He had left his .45 Colt back with Busti and felt a bit naked without it. It wasn't legal to carry a gun in some towns.

"Need a room?" the clerk asked. He was a not too tall man with a handlebar mustache. He must have had some kind of problem with his eyes that made him seem to blink a lot.

"No. What I need is some information. A few weeks ago there was a pair of white slavers here. One wore a top hat and they drink a lot of whiskey."

The clerk's eyes lit up.

"Yup. I remember them. They roughed up one of my girls and left town. Near as I can figure, they still owe me around ten dollars for damages."

"The girl still here?" asked Wil.

The clerk nodded his head.

"Mavis—get out here!" he yelled.

A woman came around the corner by the kitchen.

"Whatcha want, Elmer? I'm damned busy washing all these dishes."

"This man's looking for them two that roughed you up a few weeks ago."

"If I get hold of 'em, I'll cut 'em up bad. See this? That's where Dirk cut me."

Wil looked at the girl's arm. It was a pretty long cut.

"I need their names and where they were headed."

"Last time I saw them, they were headed for the train station," she said. "And damned good riddance to 'em."

The clerk ruffled through the pages of the register and found their names.

"Dirk Evans and Bart Hogan. Yup, that's them. They paid in cash money, in advance."

"I really appreciate the help," said Wil.

"What ya want them bums for anyway?" asked Mavis.

"They killed my wife and my mother."

Mavis and the clerk got a real sad look on their faces. It seemed so hard to believe that men could kill women with absolutely no regard for them.

Wil turned and walked back out into the sunshine.

Over a couple blocks he saw the railroad tracks and the small rail station with the name Red Wing over the door. He walked briskly across the street. When he got inside, he noticed that there were no passengers waiting and a lone clerk was listening to the clatter of a railroad telegraph.

"Oh, I didn't hear you come in. What can I do for you?" said the station master.

"I can wait until you get done with that," said Wil, pointing at the telegraph.

"Naw. That's just Herman, the station master in Omaha, telling a joke. Hold on jest a minute."

He reached over to the telegraph key and sent just a few clicks and clacks and then laughed again.

"What was that all about?" asked Wil, grinning. He seemed to be quite interested in the telegraph.

"He gets to laughing sometimes when he's sending code and makes a lot of mistakes. I just sent him 'TLF.' That means 'Now try sending code with your left foot.'"

Both men laughed for a bit.

"Now, how can I help you, mister?"

"Well, a few weeks ago, a couple men came through here

and I think they bought tickets for California." Wil dug out a scrap of paper. "Names Dirk Evans and Bart Hogan. That ring a bell?"

"I got a pretty bad memory, but I'd have records if they bought a ticket. Yup. Here 'tis. They bought tickets for San Francisco, California, and left on October 10th. From there on, it's anybody's guess."

"Thanks, mister. I reckon me and my friend will be buying the same tickets."

"Well," said the station master, "you got a while to wait. The westbound passenger train don't come 'til tomorrow morning around 7:00. Just a nosey old man askin', but what you want with them two?"

"They killed my wife and my mother."

He swallowed hard.

Wil walked back down to where Busti and Jake sat on the river bank.

"Guess we're going to take a ride on the train tomorrow. Them two got a good jump on us, but we'll still get 'em."

Busti looked at Wil and seemed to agree by just the way he looked. The two men felt serious determination and nothing was going to stop them.

Wil and Busti walked back to the hotel and rented a room for the night. The clerk was still there and agreed to store their possessions until they got back for a five-dollar bill. Wil figured that they'd be more comfortable on the river bank, but there wasn't even any water there that was fit to make a pot of coffee.

Their room was a small dimly lit place with a double bed and a washstand near the door. The wallpaper was peeling from the walls and what was left of the carpet had seen better days. All in all it would do until the morning.

During the night, Busti had to use the bathroom and he walked down the hall in the near darkness. There was only a single indoor privy on their floor and everyone had to share it.

Just as Busti got close to the door, a woman walked out into the hallway right in front of him. She looked up and saw the face of an Indian and let out a scream. She managed to wake the whole hotel and scared Busti out of a year's good living. As she continued to scream, Busti opened the bathroom door, walked in and locked the door behind him. Wil heard the commotion and kinda knew what had happened. He lay there in the light of the streetlight waiting for Busti to come back. The door opened and Busti walked in and once again shut the door behind him. Wil was grinning and Busti just threw up his hands and smiled.

"Did you hear that crazy women?"

At sunrise Wil awoke to find Busti gone, but it was no surprise to him. His friend was quite probably sitting on the bank of the river, speaking to the Great Spirit. The whole trip had been a learning experience for Busti and he had asked guidance throughout the entire trip. Now he was heading west, a place he would never have seen had it not been for the murder of his sister. He asked for courage and wisdom. It seemed that if he sat still for too long, thoughts of Flower would creep into his mind, making him feel extreme sadness. Like Wil, he was on a hunt and nothing short of killing that man would suffice.

They ate together in the hotel restaurant, ordering a large meal. They weren't too sure when they'd get to eat again. Wil ordered grits and ham and a side order of fried potatoes. Busti, not being too familiar with the written language, said that he'd take the same thing. When their meal arrived, Busti recognized the potatoes and the ham, but he wasn't too sure about the white stuff running all over his plate. He ate a path around the grits and then it was down to nothing left but that. He took his fork and tried to get a mouthful but it fell off, back onto his plate. Then he tried it with a spoon. The result was better and he took a large mouthful.

"What this?" he asked Wil.

"That's the grits you ordered."

"It look like fish eggs, but no good taste."

Wil grinned and passed him the salt and pepper and a plate of butter.

"Shake some salt and pepper on 'em. Then melt a bit of butter on top."

Busti did as instructed, and put a spoonful into his mouth.

"Still not good. Maybe I save until I get real hungry. Might taste better."

Wil laughed and slapped Busti on the shoulder.

"Some white man's food takes a while to get used to," said Wil.

After their breakfast, they packed a couple bags and headed to the train station. The station master called Wil by name and said that the train would be in on time. He was a kind man and came and sat between Wil and Busti. Wil introduced his friend and the station master offered his hand in friendship. Not many took the time to greet an Indian and Busti thought him to be a wise man of some position in his community.

There was a long drawn-out whistle as the train entered the city limits, and then they could feel its great weight shake the floor of the building. A few people got off and a large black man stepped into the station.

"We be pullin' out in five minutes," he said, looking at his watch.

Busti wondered silently what tribe he was from. He sat still watching the people come inside from the train. Some had family and loved ones waiting for them and some just stood looking around, trying to get their bearings.

Then they heard the man yell. "Board. All aboard."

Wil and Busti got on and found a pair of seats that had a window. Jake was never more than a few inches from Wil. There was a little discussion about having a dog on the train, but they eventually saw it Wil's way. There was an awful lot to see for a pair of river rats who'd never even been more than a few days away from their home. The Bigfork River would always be their home and it was a sure bet that all the people they knew had never been this far. They had to remain focused, though, on what they were doing. Their fresh grief would let them do nothing else.

Des Moines, Iowa, was their first stop other than for water and fuel once in a while. The tender always held a lot of coal, but the water went fast and they stopped frequently for more. The city was big and they had several hours until the next train heading west came through. They slept in chairs in the train station, not wanting to miss their train. Wil walked to the tobacco counter and bought a newspaper. On the front page was a picture of a small man standing with his wife and four children. He sat down next to Busti and started to read.

"What's it say?" asked Busti.

Wil started to read the story aloud. The man in the picture had been stabbed on a train as he headed for Denver, Colorado. Two men had robbed him and taken twenty dollars and change, and then they had dumped him off the train. He was the president of a big company and had been moving a large amount of cash to another bank using a cash belt. The would-be killers had missed the big money and stolen only the twenty dollars. The story continued inside the paper and Wil opened it up. There inside on the right side of the paper were the two men he had been searching for. It was an artist's drawings and didn't look much like them, but just the same, it was them. Wil looked at Busti.

"These are the men we want."

Busti nodded.

Chapter 10: Denver, Colorado

Dirk Evans and Bart Hogan spent a lot of time getting to know the back streets of Denver. When they killed the sheriff, it seemed to stir up a real hornet's nest. They had thought to get back on the train and continue their journey to California but the stations were on the lookout for the pair. Several times they had seen their pictures on the walls of restaurants and hotels. The pictures weren't that good so they still had little to worry about. The only person who had actually seen them was the woman who had been in the bar when they killed the sheriff. Dirk wanted to go back and kill her, but the heat was on them now and they didn't want to take the chance. Their money was running short and it was either get back on the train or find another grubstake. They chose the latter.

They had been staying at a downtown flophouse usually frequented by cattle men. The food was cheap and they still had over five dollars left. On one Saturday night a couple weeks after they had killed the sheriff, they were drinking whiskey with a couple cowboys. One had a pretty good amount of cash and was buying drinks for several friends. Each time he bought a round, he flashed a roll of bills. It didn't take long for Dirk to see this and the pair retreated to the alley to make a plan. The only privy was outside and behind the bar, and that's where they went to talk it over.

As the evening wore on, Dirk and Bart quit drinking and just sipped the drinks they had, trying to remain somewhat sober. Around 2:00 in the morning the place quieted down. Most of the regulars had already headed back home. The cowboy finished his drink and walked out the back door with one of his ladies of the night. He bounced off the walls once in a while and the two slavers followed at a distance, not wanting to be seen. It appeared to them that this was just too good to be true. It required nothing more than a quick knock on the head and the rest would be history.

They closed in on the cowboy and his lady and in a rush were on top of him. Dirk swung a chunk of wood at the cowboy but he ducked and moved off to his right like he'd seen it coming. The cowboy fell to the ground and pulled out a whistle, blowing it loudly. Dirk and Bart then realized that they had been set up by the law. A couple hundred feet away, a pair of lawmen were running toward them. Bart turned to run away and the cowboy reached out and caught his boot, sending him sprawling to the ground. Dirk was making time down the alley and turned at the first corner, disappearing into the night. The three lawmen had Bart in custody for attempted robbery.

Upon closer inspection the next day the lawmen discovered a warrant for the new prisoner out of Des Moines, Iowa. They had tried to kill a man on the train and dumped him outside along the tracks, more dead than alive. They still had to find Dirk Evans.

Dirk found his way back to his flophouse late the next morning. He had stolen some clothes from a clothesline and gotten a haircut. His new appearance and sober mind allowed him to blend in with the rest of the world. He made a plan to get onto the train at the Denver Station and head back to San Francisco. All he had to do was get past the law and with his new appearance, it shouldn't be too hard.

Wil and Busti had nearly had enough of day and night travel on a train. It was the same hour after hour. The conductor told them that they would be in Denver the next afternoon. The next stop for water was in eastern Colorado. Busti had taken just about all of the train ride that he could take. The constant rocking back and forth was draining on his nerves and when the train stopped on a siding to fill up with water, Busti hopped off and went for a walk. After taking on nearly a thousand gallons of water, the engineer put the big machine in gear and blew the whistle. It started down the siding and when it got back on the main rail, it started to gather speed. Busti saw it moving and started to run for the train. Just as it was getting off the siding, Busti gave a yell and reached for the railing on the caboose, running as hard as he could. The fingers of his left hand caught the rail and he pulled hard, bringing his legs up to the bottom step, his last chance to get on board. He stood on the very back of the train, his breath ragged, but with a large grin on his face.

He went into the passenger car and sat down by Wil, puffing hard.

"Now what in the hell are you grinning at?" asked Wil.

"Not much. I just went for a little run."

"Huh?" said Wil. He wasn't quite sure if he should pursue

the conversation. This was the first time he'd seen any trace of a smile on Busti in a long while.

As the train rumbled along across the countryside, Busti was amazed at the large herds of grazing antelope and mule deer. He thought of how the plains tribes must be so well fed. Again Busti started to feel like a caged animal with nowhere to run. He looked for the conductor and found him in the back car eating a sandwich.

"I want to go outside and watch the animals," said Busti.

"Sure. That's alright, but don't fall off," said the conductor, and he laughed.

Busti walked to the back of the caboose and looked around for a ladder going to the top of the train. He found it and climbed to the top. There was a flat spot on top of the car and he sat down cross-legged. The train was speeding along at over 45 miles an hour and his hair was flying everywhere. Busti turned to face the front of the train with the chill wind blowing hard into his face. The view was spectacular. He stretched out his arms as if they were wings and closed his eyes for a moment. He was sailing along on the wings of the eagle.

Again he opened his eyes and saw a golden carpet of wheat stretching from horizon to horizon. The sight was completely overwhelming. For a time he envisioned his brother the eagle swooping, diving, soaring high on the warm summer winds with Busti near his side. Truly Gitche Manitou had blessed him with this experience

The train stopped at a small station in the middle of Colorado to take on a load of coal and to top off their water tanks. The conductor told everyone that they would have an hour to get off and rest up for a while. There was a small restaurant right across the tracks from the depot and Wil thought it was time for a quick meal. They walked inside and found a table next to the window.

"Would you like a menu?" asked the waitress. "Coffee?"

"Sure," said Wil.

Busti couldn't read the menu so Wil made some suggestions for him. They decided to each have a big steak with potatoes and gravy as long as it didn't take too long. Then they saw the engineers walk in. As long as they kept an eye on those guys, they wouldn't be left behind. The meal was pretty good and they even had time for pie.

As they walked outside, they heard the conductor yell "all aboard" and the train whistle blew loudly. It started to move and once again Busti was running for the train with Wil right beside him. They managed to catch the caboose as it went by but had a little trouble getting Jake to jump up. Wil found the conductor and asked him what had happened. The engineers were still eating their meal across the road.

"Dis is where the train crews change," he told them.

This traveling by rail was new for both of them and if they were to get to their destination, they had better stick closer to the train.

The train was gathering speed and the conductor was once again checking tickets. He and Busti had started to become friends. When he had finished his duties, he stopped by Busti and asked him if he wanted to have coffee with him in the caboose.

"I got a pot going in back," said the conductor.

"Thanks. I like coffee," said Busti.

They walked back through an empty passenger car, through the baggage car and then into the caboose. Walking on a moving floor was difficult, but Busti was starting to get the hang of it. The conductor poured them each a cup and Busti fixed it the way he liked it with a lot of sugar, a rare treat on the river. Then they went through the next door and out onto a railed part of the caboose. There were two padded chairs and a small table to set the coffee cups on. The scenery was spectacular, speeding by at over 45 miles an hour. Busti was again most impressed.

"My name's Ben. What's yours?" asked the conductor.

"I am Bustikogan, but some call me Busti." He slurped his coffee loudly.

"Well, Busti, it's good to meet you. There's not many folk who will take the time to talk to a black man nowadays."

"Not many folk wanna talk to a big Indian either," Busti said, and the two laughed.

"Where ya from?"

"Far from here on the Bigfork River."

"What state is that?"

"Minnesota, I think. I never go to school."

"Whoee. Now that's a long way from here!"

"We been on the trail for many days and have far to go."

"I see yur headin' for San Francisco. That's a long trip for anyone. What ya doin' there?"

"Some bad men kill my sister and now I look for them. When I find them, I cut them in small pieces and feed them to the ravens. My friend Wil took her for wife."

The conductor was a bit surprised at the anger in Busti's voice and on his face.

"We see the pictures in the paper where they kill a passenger for twenty dollars."

The conductor got a most serious look on his face. "Wait here," said the conductor.

He went inside and came out with a Denver newspaper.

"That was my train. Those guys stabbed one of my passengers. Here. Look at this."

He held open the *Denver Post* and there was a picture of the two men.

"That's them," said Busti. "What words say?"

"It says that they arrested Bart Hogan in Denver while he was trying to rob an undercover officer. I'm not sure what that is, though," said the conductor.

Busti got a slight smile on his face. "We on good trail," said Busti.

They sat for several hours watching as the countryside changed from flat to rolling hills. The two were becoming friends.

"Ever seen a mountain?" asked Ben.

"Not know what a mountain is."

"Come with me, Busti. We'll go up front so you can see one."

Ben lead Busti once again through the train, past Wil sleeping in a corner and outside through the tender car. They came through one small door and the noise nearly knocked Busti off the train. Ben motioned for Busti to bend down and he yelled into his ear. "This is the engine and that man is shoveling coal into the firebox to make steam."

The engineer looked a bit nervous seeing a real live Indian right next to him.

"Look over the top of the smoke stack. That's the Rocky Mountains. Tomorrow we'll be going right through them and that will take us a long time," said Ben.

Busti was impressed, but more so with the engine. There were many brass control rods and valves as well as glass-covered gauges, and steam leaked out everywhere. Ben motioned for Busti to follow him again into the caboose.

"Much noise in there. My ears are making a ringing sound," said Busti.

"Ya. Most of the engineers are deaf from the noise. It's a hard job."

Over the course of several hours, the two became close friends. Ben learned how Busti had been taken as a slave and Busti learned how Ben's father had been a slave too. There were many miles between where they had lived, but their histories were quite similar. Slavery was the word that gave them common ground. Ben's father had been one of the last slaves freed and Busti had grown up a slave until his escape back on the river. The men he sought were slavers too. Ben told of how his relatives had been taken from Africa and brought to America in chains on the great sailing ships.

"There ya are," said Wil. "I thought you'd fallen off the train."

"We just passin' time," said Ben. "Here. Take a look at this."

Wil read the article about the men they hunted. "Looks like we're on the right trail, Busti."

Chapter 11: Hot Trail

Dirk Evans still was doing his best to survive.
He stole from drunks at night and took purses from old ladies
when nobody was around to help them. Still inside his pants
pocket, he held a train ticket stub for San Francisco. He holed
up in his flophouse room most of the daytime and hunted at
night. Still, he was a fierce predator and would kill for even
the smallest gain. The Denver police had posters up in nearly
every bar and hotel. The drawing of him didn't do him justice,
though, since he had gotten a haircut and some new clothes.
His biggest problem was getting back on the train without
being recognized.

On one particularly cold Denver day, his money had run
out and he was forced to look for work. Even the flophouse
had thrown his possessions out into the street. He had seen an
advertisement in the paper for a black crew, moving coal in

the rail yards. They paid every day and the going rate was twenty cents an hour. He wasn't used to hard labor but figured it might get him through his hard times.

As he worked one day, he noticed that the westbound passenger train filled its tender car there for the trip through the mountains. It went from the rail station to the coal yard and each day it was always on the same schedule. The railroads all prided themselves on being on time. He was to start work at 9:00 a.m. and work until 7:00 p.m. when the last train for the day left. After two weeks, he had his plan set. The westbound train left at 7:30 a.m. and when nobody was looking, he'd get on board and sit down with the passengers. This would let him avoid the eyes of the law in the big terminal.

He had saved a few dollars from his labor on the coal piles and if he was careful, it might be enough to get him to California. The police had been at his hotel the day before and put a wanted poster up on the bulletin board. He removed it as soon as he saw it.

■■■ ■■ ■■■

Wil and Busti arrived in Denver near dark and found a nearby hotel for the night. The clerk had tried to get Busti and Jake to find a different place for the night, but Wil convinced him otherwise. It seemed that people just hated anyone who looked different from themselves.

After settling in, they went down to the restaurant for dinner. Wil picked up a paper, looking for anything that could help in their search. San Francisco was a long way off. As he sat going through the paper, a waitress came and handed them menus. Again Wil had to give Busti some help with the reading. It seemed that the prices were pretty high, and a steak was well over a dollar. It felt good to have an ample supply of money in his pockets. So far they had spent way over thirty-five dollars and the end wasn't yet in sight.

While waiting for their dinner, Wil paged through the paper. Then he saw the face of the man he wanted. A chill went down his back and anger raised up close to the surface. The man in the top hat was in jail in Denver and they'd go see him the next day.

Morning arrived after a fitful night spent in a city hotel. They had planned to stay only a day but after reading the paper last night, they paid for an additional two days. Wil would need time to sort it all out. They had breakfast in the same restaurant and again picked up the morning paper. There it was again, another story on the men who had tried to kill a nice family man on the train. It was complete with pictures and a plea for anyone who saw the fugitive to come forward. They ate their meal in a hurry and walked out into the street to find the police station. It was nearly two miles to the uptown station. A snowy wind was blowing into their faces, and the trip reminded them both of Minnesota.

Wil had left his .45 Colt in his room and hid his knife inside his pants. Busti kept his knife hidden up by his armpit. Even with all the armed police around, Wil felt the need to arm himself. They walked into a large granite building and saw a policemen sitting behind a big desk.

"Just a minute. I gotta finish this complaint," said the officer.

Wil and Busti sat down on a bench, looking around at the high walls and the picture of President Roosevelt. The whole place had an official feel to it.

"Alright now. What can I do for you lads?" asked the officer.

Wil opened up the paper and showed him the picture of the fugitive.

"Him and another guy killed my wife and mother."

The officer became quite interested in what Wil had to say. "Come right this way," said the officer, and he led them down the hall. "This is Sergeant Anderson."

Sergeant Anderson stood up and offered his hand to Wil and then in turn to Busti.

"Have a seat, gentlemen. Now tell me what I can do for you."

Wil started talking and didn't quit for nearly ten minutes. He told about Sum Chi and Flower, and how he had found her murdered. He spoke of how his mother had been killed when he was so young. He told of his relationship with Busti and how he and Flower had been used as slaves by another clan. He told of their trip to Denver, searching as they went.

Wil got quiet for a bit, thinking of how he would personally kill those men.

"Sounds to me like we have exactly half of the men you're looking for right upstairs locked up. There's still quite an investigation going because of that attempted murder on the train and when we arrested Hogan, he was trying to kill one of my best men. Do you want to go up and look at him?" asked the sergeant.

Wil nodded and they all started walking down a long hall and then up three flights of stairs. The jailer let them in and then they walked down another long cell-lined hall.

"Here he is. Is that the man?"

Wil looked at him and at first wasn't quite sure. Then recognition flooded his mind. All he had to do was imagine the man's face wearing a top hat. This was the man who had sold Sum Chi to him. This was one of the white slavers. This was the most hated of men, the bastard who had killed his mother. This was Bart Hogan, the man they had chased for so many miles.

Wil and Busti backed away from the cell and talked quietly for a moment and at the same time, the sergeant advised Hogan who Busti and Wil were. He laughed for a bit and Wil looked over at him.

"What the hell does he think is so funny?" asked Wil.

"I used that little China girl every which way I could for over two years. She was pretty good too. I musta sold her a dozen times. Made quite a bit of money from her too. As for your mommy, she was a weakling. She closed her eyes while I raped her and forgot to open them again," said Hogan with a sadistic grin.

The slaver continued to talk and laugh and it was aimed directly at the hearts of both Wil and Busti. He listened carefully and fully understood what the man said. He was the man who had brought Sum Chi up to the Bigfork to be sold and resold. As the man continued to laugh Busti's anger grew, filling him to overflowing. Wil and Sergeant Anderson were at the cell bars and Busti stood behind them looking at Hogan. Slowly Busti reached inside his shirt and put his hand on the shank of his knife. He got a good grip on it and pulled it out. In one fluid motion his arm came back and then with the fury of hell itself, he let the knife fly toward the man's heart. It was as if the whole thing was happening in slow motion. The knife made a single rotation so that the blade went forward and then, just as it went over Sergeant Anderson's head, it touched the cell bars and clattered to the floor doing no damage. Anderson drew his snub-nosed Colt and aimed it at Busti. Jake let out a low growl.

"Now that will be about all of that I'm gonna take from you, chief."

Then he turned to Hogan.

"Guess you got somebody looking out for you today, mister."

He turned the gun on Hogan and told him to kick the knife over to him. Hogan was shaking badly and had a hard time getting up from his chair. His worthless life would yet go on for a while but not because Busti wanted it to. This low-life had treated his wife badly and then sold her many times. His hatred was strong and would not be denied.

They walked back downstairs and the sergeant filled out appropriate the complaint papers. This insured that Hogan would never go free, and if convicted, would surely hang from the gallows. There was no mention made of Busti trying to stick a knife in that man's heart.

The sergeant, Busti and Wil talked for quite a while and Sergeant Anderson seemed to think that the other slaver Dirk Evans had found a way out of town. The police department hadn't heard anything for quite a while. Normally the local bartenders knew about any strangers, but there was nothing new to go on.

"Here's your knife, Busti. I know you'd like to stick that bastard, but then I'd have to hang you too," said the sergeant.

As they walked out of the police station, Busti asked Wil, "What is bastard?"

The next train heading for San Francisco was at 7:30 the next morning. Wil figured they had better keep on the trail before it got cold and Evans was gone forever. The search for Flower's killer now had a sense of urgency. With one out of the way, it might be a bit more difficult to find him. People don't even look up at a single person, but they do notice a pair. Information would be hard to come by.

Wil and Busti were up way before daylight and had breakfast downstairs. They knew it might be the last good meal they would have for awhile. Trains sometimes didn't stop for long distances. At 6:30, they were at the train station in downtown Denver. The train still had to be loaded with coal, but this would happen after the passengers got on. It had been a full week since they had been on the train and Wil recognized one of the engineers from last week. Then Busti saw his friend Ben. Their eyes met and they walked toward each other like long-lost friends. The big black man extended his hand to Busti and they talked for a while.

"Good to see you, my friend Busti."

"I not think I see you again."

"Are you two going to finish your trip to San Francisco?"

"Yup. We did find one of the slavers, though, and he's in jail right down the street," said Wil. "He might just die right here in Denver on the end of a rope."

"I gotta get to work, but we'll have coffee later. Alright, Busti?" asked Ben.

Busti nodded and grinned at the big black man.

In time, the conductor started to board the passengers.

"Board. All aboard," called Ben.

The train held over forty people, but that morning there was only thirteen. Ben had been counting the passengers and checking their tickets. Then when it was time to pull out, he went to the passenger car and stood at the back counting. He came up with fourteen, one more than he had counted at the boarding platform. Regulations said that he had to go now from one passenger to the next and check their tickets. That done, he just figured that he had missed one, which was not likely, though, after so many years doing this.

The engineer gave a couple short pulls on the steam whistle and the train moved ahead slowly to the coal yard. The loading only took about five minutes. Then they moved slowly out of the siding onto the main rail. The engineer checked his watch and proceeded to push forward on the throttle. The massive steamer came to life and the wheels slipped for just a moment. Then the big machine started to gather speed on the main rail. The whistle screamed wildly into the morning sky and the train left the Denver rail yard, threading its way westward into the Rocky Mountains.

So far the trip had gone smoothly. Wil had the pleasure of seeing the man who had killed his mother in custody with no hope that he'd ever be set free. He still had blood in his eye, though, and wasn't quite sure what he'd do if he caught up to the other man. He thought he'd probably kill him, but he still wasn't sure how. Way down inside, he swore that his hatred would not be denied. The sergeant at the station had warned both of them that if they took the law into their own hands, they'd have to stand trial for it. No man was above the law, even in a case like this. Damn the law. He had to kill this lowlife himself and no matter the consequences, he would. Busti seemed satisfied to just get him hung, but with Wil it had gotten deep into his soul.

As the train rolled gently from side to side, it gave Wil a time to remember how happy he had been back on the river. He thought of how Flower had brought him breakfast while he was sitting outside watching the sun come up one morning. They sat together quietly watching the colors of summer brighten in the morning sun.

He thought of when they had first moved into their cabin. Flower and Wil discovered love together and it seemed that they made love each time they came close to each other. He would walk near her and she would take his arm, drawing him down to the soft grass and holding him tightly. At first there was a strong sense of urgency and then as they became so much closer, their lovemaking slowed, as they took time to discover each other.

And then there was the time he had gotten sick from some bad meat. Flower tended him when he was near death, not moving more than a few feet from him. She loved him deeply and showed it in many ways each day. Now there was nothing left for him. He had to find Dirk Evans.

Jake usually slept curled up near Wil's feet, but today he seemed to be a bit nervous. He kept his head on Wil's leg or was busy watching the other passengers.

Ben and Busti eventually found their way to the back of the train.

"These are the prettiest mountains there is, Busti. Look how high they go," said Ben, pointing skyward..

The little train was moving through the mountains, going higher all the time.

"I never see this before," Busti said. Busti enjoyed being outside, away from the smell of the passengers.

"In a couple hours, we go through a big tunnel. Then we have to go inside or the smoke will kill us."

Busti's eyes got big thinking about a tunnel big enough for a train.

Ben was going through some papers as they went along and Busti asked him if there was some kind of trouble.

"Well," said Ben, "when the passengers got on, I counted 'em. Den when they sat down in they seats, I counted 'em again. There was one more the second count. I jiss don't know where that udder one came from."

Busti laughed at Ben.

"Maybe he sneaked on when you wasn't lookin," said Busti.

"I already thought about that, but everybody has a ticket."

They rode along in silence for quite a while, just enjoying the colors of the mountains and their coffee.

"Time to head back in, Busti. That tunnel isn't too far from here."

They walked back inside and Busti sat down next to Wil. Jake wagged his tail and licked Busti's hand.

"Can I have your attention, please? In a few minutes, we'll be going through a tunnel. You'll have to keep da windows and doors closed 'til we get on the udder side to keep da smoke out."

A couple hours later, Ben motioned for Busti to come back to the caboose again.

"I got it, Busti. After we stop for water and a meal, I'm going to check tickets again. All dem passengers bought their tickets in Denver and the date'll be stamped on 'em. If I have any trouble, I'll need you to help me. I'm getting a little old for rassling' with passengers."

The train slowed some and then came to a stop in a little gold town high in the mountains.

"We's takin on water and coal for an hour, so you have time to go and get a quick meal," said Ben.

The passengers all got off the train and walked to the café a short distance away. Even Jake felt relieved to get out for a while. Wil and Busti ate a quick sandwich and then got back on the train, not wanting to be left behind.

As boarding time neared, everyone got back on and took their same seats. The train started moving once more, going quite slowly out of the town.

"Folks, I gotta check your tickets again so have 'em ready when I come around," said Ben.

He started at the back and made a quick count with the same result. He still was having trouble thinking that he had miscounted. He checked several tickets and when he got to a man in back who was looking out the window, he had to ask twice to see his ticket. The man appeared to be quite agitated and didn't want to show his ticket. Busti started to move closer to Ben in case of trouble and all at once the man jumped up, grabbing Ben around his throat.

Busti moved quickly to help his friend and Wil was coming from the other side. The man looked trapped.

"Git back or so help me, I'll stick this nigger," said Evans.

The light of recognition burned brightly in Wil Morgan's mind. Here was the slaver they had been chasing for so many miles. This was Dirk Evans, the man who had murdered Flower. He had an arm around Ben's chest and a knife at his throat. There was a moment when he just wanted to get at him, but then moment by moment, common sense took over. Wil and Busti were no more than five feet from them but it was almost a sure thing that Ben would get killed in the process. Wil stared intently at Evans, trying to burn his face into his mind forever. This hunt wasn't over yet.

Each time he tried to move with Ben, Jake would growl and the women in the car would scream. The whole situation was tense.

"Now git back, dammit," said Evans.

They followed him down the aisle toward the caboose. He

moved slowly with Ben right next to him. When they came to the door of the caboose, Evans found it locked.

"Gimme the damned key!"

"Yessir. It's on my key chain," said Ben.

Still Wil and Busti were only a few feet away.

Ben unlocked the door and they went into the caboose, closing the door behind them. Then they heard the key in the lock again. Wil reached for the handle and it was locked, with Evans and Ben on the other side.

Wil hurried back forward and found a way to get up on top of the car with Busti right behind him. Just as they reached the back of the caboose, they heard a low yell and Evans jumped off the train, rolling in the loose gravel. By the time they got to Ben, he was bleeding badly from a bad cut to his arm.

"Can you take care of him?" Wil asked Busti.

His arm was in pretty bad condition.

Wil went over the rail of the speeding rail car and down the steps near the tracks. Evans was already a long way back. He gave a hard push and hit the gravel feet first, sliding downward. The train was slowing, but that didn't help Wil much. He had several cuts on his legs and on his head. The hunt was still on.

Wil climbed back up on the rails and started to take inventory. He still had his knife, but more importantly, he had his Colt .45. He had no serious injuries so he made the decision to chase Evans down. He looked down the rails and saw that the train had stopped nearly a mile away. He went back further on the tracks until he saw where Evans had hit the gravel. Now Wil was in his own element. The woodsman, the hunter and the tracker all came out at once and his determination grew.

The chase went on for many hours and it seemed that Wil wasn't gaining on Evans at all. He came to a stream and kneeled down to get a drink of mountain water. He heard a sound and braced himself for the worst. A big yellow dog nearly knocked him over. Jake had found him and when he looked up he saw his friend Busti coming his way too. The help might just be needed. They sat for a short while trying to catch their breath. The mountain altitude was wearing hard on them all. Evans was driven by fear of being caught and Wil was driven by hatred. It was a tossup who would outlast the other.

The trail led down through a small valley. Wil looked ahead and saw something shimmering in the sunlight. As he walked on, it became apparent that he was seeing a small cabin. He quickened his pace some. As he got closer, a man walked out.

"You seen a bald-headed man come through here in the last hour?" asked Wil.

"Nope. I ain't."

The man looked a bit scared.

"Ya sure?" asked Wil.

"Now jiss git outta here. This is private land," said the old man.

"Alright," said Wil.

They walked back down the trail and as soon as they were out of sight, they moved into the trees.

"There's another man inside," said Busti. "Did you see the way Jake was sniffing the door?"

"Yup, but he's probably got a gun aimed right at the old man and he can't talk."

"We just gotta wait 'til he comes out," said Wil. "Then I'll shoot him."

Busti looked at Wil, not liking what he saw. The kind and gentle man had blood in his eye and wanted vengeance for the murder of Flower. It didn't seem that there was much that would stop him.

Wil and Busti sat in the treeline watching the little cabin for signs of life. Then as darkness started to overtake the little valley, he saw the door open just a short way. Evans stepped out and looked around. He seemed to be a bit more at ease now. The men who were chasing him were nowhere in sight. He carried what appeared to be a 30-30 saddle carbine. He walked behind the little cabin and in a few minutes went back inside.

"I think that the only way we'll get him is to burn him out, but then we might kill the old man too. We just can't take that chance," said Wil.

"How 'bout we just plug up the chimney and smoke him out?" asked Busti.

"You get close to the cabin and put a rag on the stove pipe. I'll shoot him when he comes out," said Wil.

Busti looked at Wil again and saw the raging hatred in his eyes.

Wil was in position and Busti quietly placed a piece of cloth over the pipe. In just a short time, he heard them coughing and the door opened with Evans coming out first.

Wil grabbed the man and tumbled him hard to the ground. He drew his knife and placed it none too gently on the slaver's throat. The Colt .45 was far to impersonal. All that was left on this trail for revenge was to push the knife down and slide it to the side. The man had his eyes wide open in fear and knew that his time was nearly over. Now he would pay for all of the bad things he had done, but especially for the murder of Wil's wife, Flower.

Wil's hand started to shake and then he rolled off Evans chest. Revenge was one thing, but cold murder just wasn't inside him. The real Wil Morgan came out and for this most hated of men, it wasn't a moment too soon. Busti was right next to Wil and could have stopped him from killing Evans, but this was Wil's decision and he would not interfere.

Busti sat the man up and tied his hands behind him. The trail had ended. The man they had searched for was sitting on the ground with tears falling from his eyes. The coward was such a brave man when it came to killing a woman, but now he cried like a little girl.

The old man inside the cabin came out in a short while, looking a bit worse for wear. Old Jimmy had been panning gold for a long time here in the mountains and very rarely had anyone shown up to talk to. He looked down at Evans and kicked him in the ribs.

"You bastard. The first company I get in two years and ya gotta be a bad one. Damnation!"

Wil and Busti laughed. The hatred that drove Wil on his hunt had left him. He'd made the decision to let the law do the punishing. For the first time in many weeks, he felt at ease. The trail had ended.

"Can ya put us up for the night, mister?" asked Wil.

"Why shore I kin. I got beans and bacon and I make the best damned biscuits in the entire valley." The old man laughed. He was the only resident for many miles.

They ate and talked deep into the night and by morning it was time to hit the trail to the nearest town. The old man had treated them well and even Jake got a good meal.

"How's the hunting around here?" asked Wil.

"Well mister, we got elk that are so big they'll scare ya. When them big boys start bugling, it's something you'll never forget."

Wil's eyes lit up. "What do you think about going hunting sometime next fall?"

"Why shore! I'll go hunting any time. Lot more fun than looking for gold too," said the old man.

They all spent quite a bit of time talking hunting and Wil told him all about the lakes and rivers of Minnesota. When he got to the part about the really big fish, the old man asked if Wil would show him how to catch some next spring. They were all getting to be good friends.

The town was over five miles away and it took quite a while to walk there. When they straggled into town, a prisoner in ropes behind them, it didn't take long for the police to catch up with them.

Wil told the story of how they had tracked Evans across four states for murdering his wife and mother and it seemed that the officer already knew about him. The story of cutting Ben the conductor's arm was getting around too. He'd survive, but would have to take some time off from the railroad. Busti handed the rope to the policeman and they all followed him to the station. The chase was over.

The Denver police sent a detective to pick up the prisoner and gave Busti, Wil, and Jake a ride to the train station. Wil pulled out a roll of bills and paid for their tickets. Still seemed like a lot of money just to ride on a train. It was getting on toward mid-December and all of the lakes and rivers would be frozen back in northern Minnesota. He still had to stop and get his gear that he'd left in Red Wing and then he had to buy another ticket to International Falls, not too far from his home on the river.

They boarded the eastbound train and found a spot to get comfortable. Jake had his head across Wil's leg. The trip would take several days. Wil's thoughts turned to the river. His home was gone now and that bothered him some. It was already too cold to set up a winter camp. He had a few choices, though. He could spend the winter trapping with Busti or maybe spend the season with Sam Three Toes and his family. He closed his eyes for a while. He grinned slightly thinking about Fawn and little Gray Duck. It would be good to see them all again.

Busti and Wil were heading home. Their trail had come to an end. Busti thought of his bride Sum Chi. Wil sat with his eyes closed trying to remember Flower's face. He had had a lot of time to think in the last few weeks and had decided to go back to his place on the Waboose. Busti would still be his neighbor and would most certainly help him build a new home. Life could still be good for him; he was still young.

As the train chugged along toward International Falls, Minnesota, they crossed a stream with open water, somewhat unusual for the cold weather of this area. There in the middle of this small spot of open water was a large duck paddling slowly in circles, a kind of gray-looking duck.

Wil reached down and put his hand on Jake's head.

Printed in the United States
30675LVS00002BA/106-114